I0543447

A DOOMED REUNION

Also by Alice Zogg

Stand-Alone Mysteries

A Lethal Joke
A Dark Book Club
A Bad Apple
Exposing the Past
No Curtain Call
The Ill-Fated Scientist
Accidental Eyewitness
A Bet Turned Deadly

R. A. Huber Mysteries

Evil at Shore Haven
Guilty or Not
Murder at the Cubbyhole
Revamp Camp
Final Stop Albuquerque
The Fall of Optimum House
The Lonesome Autocrat
Tracking Backward
Turn the Joker Around
Reaching Checkmate

A DOOMED REUNION

ALICE ZOGG

This book is a work of fiction.

Copyright © 2024, Alice Zogg
First Edition

Without limiting the rights under copyright reserved above, no
part of this publication may be reproduced, stored in or introduced
into a retrieval system, or transmitted, in any form or by any means
(electronic, mechanical, photocopying, recording, or otherwise),
without the prior written permission of the copyright owner of this book.

Published by Aventine Press
55 East Emerson St.
Chula Vista CA 91911
www.aventinepress.com

ISBN: 978-1-955162-33-3
Library of Congress Control Number: 2024911636
Library of Congress Cataloging-in-Publication Data
A Doomed Reunion/Alice Zogg
Printed in the United States of America

ALL RIGHTS RESERVED

In memory of Walter, our family friend for many decades

CREDITS

Lars Larsson educated me about Southern California's jockeys and race track industry of 30 years ago, as opposed to now. Thank you, Lars. Not having grown up or been schooled in the United States, I was unfamiliar with what happened at high school class reunions. Besides food, was there entertainment and dancing, I wondered? Thanks are in order to my daughter Andrea, who enlightened me that the main activity at a reunion decades after high school is to touch base with former classmates and reminisce about the school years. I gave my characters a dark event to reminisce over. Once again, daughter Franziska applied herself to proofreading my manuscript. I would not dare to write without being able to count on her skill. Kudos are also in order to Gayle Bartos-Pool for an excellent editing job. Last, but not least, I appreciate the patience of my husband, Wilfried, as I vanished into the computer room, oblivious to the world.

As to the location of the fictional town of Seabreeze, I took the liberty and placed it between Del Mar and La Jolla.

CAST OF CHARACTERS

Sister Margaret (Angie Cadieux)	A nun; organized the class reunion
Lori Aames-Winter	A former homecoming queen; is still a beauty
Ray Winter	Lori's husband; CIO of a large company
Heather Jones-Levine	A retail buyer; was a bit wild in her schooldays
Jacob Levine	Heather's husband; feels out of place
Alex Kazarian	Owns a car wash business; talks about it with pride
Michelle Kazarian	Alex's wife; is not thrilled to attend the reunion
Raphael Torres	A jockey; used to get bullied in school
Lucia Torres	Raphael's wife; a Latin dancer
Dong Kim	A scientist; was known in high school as *Gray Matter*
Chin Sun Kim	Dong's wife; is also a scientist
Martin Taylor	A pianist; tends to be a bit high strung
Vito Taylor	Martin's husband; has a calming effect on his spouse
Dean Rickey	A programmer; unloads a bombshell
Gigi	Dean's hired escort
Justin Picard	Fell to his death 30 years ago
Detective Scharfkopf	Investigating officer of the San Diego County Sheriff's Department

PROLOGUE

At the beginning of March sister Margaret had a conversation with Mother Superior at the convent of the Sisters of Temperance, located in San Diego, California. The conversation went as follows:

Mother Superior: You do understand that upon entering the convent you took the vows of poverty, which forbids personal wealth?

Sister Margaret: I'm aware of that, Your Reverence. The bulk of my inheritance will benefit the convent - - and I specifically bequeath it to our overseas missions - - but with a small portion, I would like to finance my 30-year high school class reunion.

Mother Superior: Your former classmates could not afford to attend?

Sister Margaret: Oh, I'm sure they could, but I would like to treat them.

Mother Superior: When would the reunion be?

Sister Margaret: In the fall.

Mother Superior: You are committed to serve in our Asian missions starting in the fall of this year.

Sister Margaret: I will make sure to schedule the reunion prior to my departure.

Mother Superior thought about it for a long moment and then announced, "Since this endeavor does not benefit you personally but rather all the people in your high school class, you have my blessing."

Six months later

CHAPTER 1

On Saturday evening, September 7, Lori and Ray Winter were driving to Lori's class reunion held at a resort hotel by the ocean in their town called Seabreeze. The small community was nestled between Del Mar and La Jolla, a mere 15-mile drive from San Diego. Amid a curving coastline, Seabreeze boasted rocky shores to the east and a sandy beach to the west. The Winters lived only three miles farther inland. Theoretically, they could have walked.

Lori said, "I know you're not thrilled about attending but please try to be charming for my sake."

Ray took his eyes off the road for an instant and, glancing her way, replied, "I'll be on my best behavior but I don't understand why we are going. We avoided your 10th and 20th reunion, so what's so special about this one?"

"To refresh your memory, during the first one I was giving birth to our twins, and the next one was held while we were vacationing in Europe. As for what's so special about today's reunion, it's the fact that Angie has organized it and is even paying everyone's way. You well know that Angie was my best friend in high school and still is."

"So what prompts dear Sister Margaret to be so generous with her money? And more to the point, isn't she supposed to have given up all worldly goods?"

"Don't be sarcastic, Ray. When her parents passed away this year, she inherited a fortune. I happen to know that she is donating the bulk of it to the convent, but this reunion is sort of a good-bye to her past. She is scheduled to leave for work in a foreign mission soon and may never return to the US."

At this point they had reached the hotel, which ended their conversation.

At roughly the same time, Heather Jones-Levine and her husband, Jacob, were driving to Seabreeze from San Diego. Heather had attended her 10-year reunion - - a big bash with a live band, dancing, and formal attire - - with her first husband. Ten years ago, on her 20th , she showed up alone. Now she was about to arrive on the arm of Jacob, her current husband, who was 12 years her junior.

He said, "Am I expected to contribute to anything?"

"Don't worry, Hon, I'm sure it'll be low key," she replied.

"What does that mean?"

"Probably no music and dancing. Only food, drink, and a bunch of us catching up about our lives. Of course we'll also talk about our high school days."

"That's what I'm afraid of. I'll feel out of place."

"Not at all! I bet the women will be jealous of my good-looking husband," and she nudged him playfully.

Jacob murmured under his breath, "Like a trophy hubby," as they pulled into the hotel parking lot.

Raphael Torres and spouse Lucia headed over from Del Mar on Pacific Coast Highway. As they reached the small town, Raphael decided to take a detour a bit inland and drive through the neighborhood he had grown up in. The humble two-bedroom rental house his family had occupied was barely recognizable due to many additions and alterations. Then he drove by the high school building. When parallel with Seabreeze High, he slowed the car to a walking pace and then stopped along the curb.

Dusk had set in but the school grounds were well illuminated. One-story buildings housed the classrooms and a centralized two-story structure accommodated the auditorium, cafeteria, and teacher's lounge. It was anyone's guess what the architect had in mind when adding a turret to that building at the center of the complex. The gym had its own, separate location.

Raphael said, "Nothing seems to have changed here in the last few decades."

"Are you feeling nostalgic with good memories?" Lucia wanted to know.

"Some, but not all were good."

He did not immediately explain, and so she waited.

He stared up at the odd turret for a moment and then continued, "I was made fun of and bullied because I didn't smell good at times when I came to school straight from the stables without having time to shower."

"I don't understand. You were not a jockey until after high school."

"Yes, but I was helping out at ranches, cleaning stalls, grooming and exercising the horses, early in the mornings."

"How come you never told me about this?"

"It's not important; over and done with decades ago."

She reached over and touched his hand, saying, "I'm sorry the boys bullied you."

"It was only one guy, most of the time. The star football player."

"I hope he doesn't come to the reunion."

She could not see the grin on his face in the dark as Raphael stated, "There is no chance of that."

Martin and Vito Taylor lived in Escondido and were driving along the I-15 South freeway when Vito commented, "I'm impressed that your folks could afford a house in Seabreeze."

"We were not rich; you've got that right. Seabreeze was a different place then. When I grew up, it was a modest small town with a population of mostly middle-income class families. It has only become an affluent spot, boasting high-end real estate, in the last two decades," his husband replied.

They were driving in silence for a couple of miles before Vito asked the next question. "Are we going to shock folks this evening?"

"What?"

"You told me once that you had not 'come out' until after high school."

"True. I was not openly gay yet, but people knew."

"Did the kids make fun of you?"

"Most did not, except for one boy. I was terrified of him, and he usually kept a flock of buddies around."

"If he remembers you tonight, he'll probably feel bad about it and may even apologize," remarked Vito.

"Too late for that; he's dead."

CHAPTER 2

Alex and Michelle Kazarian stayed at the hotel for two nights in order not to have to drive back to Glendale late at night on Saturday. They also wanted to take advantage of visiting San Diego.

While getting ready in their room, Alex closed the lobster clasp of Michelle's necklace, then remarked, "You look great in your new dress."

Michelle did a last quick check in the mirror, touched up her lipstick and then replied, "Thanks, but I can't get enthused about going to your shindig. I'll be bored to tears having to sit through everyone talking about your school days."

"Look at it this way. It's a night out and we'll get a free meal," he joked.

As they headed for the door, Michelle had the last word, saying, "I've heard that in many European countries spouses are not invited to class reunions, which makes a lot of sense."

In a room a few doors down the hotel corridor, Dong Kim and Chin Sun Kim were also getting ready for the party. Both were second-generation Koreans, born in the USA.

Chin Sun said, "I'm so glad you suggested making a vacation at the beach out of this. The hotel is lovely; the entire town is, what I've seen of it so far."

Her husband replied, "That's the least I can do for you since you won't know anyone at the reunion. We'll have a great few days here exploring the town, swimming, snorkeling, or simply relaxing."

Then he chuckled and added, "I may not recognize people myself, as I'm sure they've changed in 30 years."

"You'll recognize Sister Margaret dressed in her habit."

He stated, "She was Angie in high school and I took her to the senior prom."

That made Chin Sun giggle as they stepped out of their hotel door.

Dean Rickey stayed at a modest bed and breakfast place about half a mile from the ocean. He lived in Tucson, Arizona, but with any luck, anticipated to relocate back to his hometown of Seabreeze.

He checked his watch. It was time to pick up his escort. He was planning to get to the reunion a bit late and make a grand entrance.

CHAPTER 3

Sister Margaret, wearing a name tag that said "Angie Cadieux," greeted her guests at the entrance of the large hotel hall. She directed them to the check-in desk and announced to the arrivals, "Welcome! Please sign the guest book. Classmates, go ahead and grab a name tag and print your name on it. Maiden names only. No need for spouses to do so."

Large round tables were set up with white tablecloths, silverware, and goblets throughout the huge hall, seating 15 people each. A bouquet of yellow and white roses - - their school colors - - garnished every table as the centerpiece. No one sat down yet, but stood in groups and mingled as more folks joined in. Some social butterflies had not lost their touch and floated from group to group.

Wearing name tags was a good idea as peoples' appearance had changed over the years. Especially the men's hairlines had either receded or their manes had turned gray. Some classmates were heavier and others had thinned since their school years.

Angie was announcing that there was no assigned seating and that people were welcome to choose any table, when Dean and his date arrived.

As they entered the hall, Dean draped an arm firmly around his date's shoulder and called out, "Hello everyone, I'm Dean Rickey, and please meet my friend Gigi."

Gigi - - 21 years old, blonde, 5'9," and wearing three-inch heels - - towered over him. She wriggled out of his hold and hissed under her breath, "I told you, touching is extra, so keep your hands to yourself."

Angie could not help smiling, but nobody else paid attention. They were all preoccupied with catching up with their peers.

Dean's grandiose entrance had not gone down as planned, but he recovered fast and turned to Angie, saying, "Thanks for your generosity. I see you're ditching being a nun for the occasion."

"If you mean the habit, I never wore one," she returned. "It has not been mandatory for sisters to wear habits for decades. As for the rest of your remark, I'm not ditching anything."

Gigi asked, "Do we address you with 'Your Grace' or something?"

The former smiled at her and replied, "Just Angie, please."

As people started to get seated, Lori guided Ray to Angie's table, making sure she would sit next to her friend. Dean also gravitated to the same round table. Soon the hotel personnel came on the scene, asking each person's preference of beef, fish, or vegetarian, and red wine, white wine, or beer.

While they were waiting for their food, Angie took the initiative and asked, "Who attended earlier reunions?"

Heather said, "I showed up for both, the 10th and 20th." Martin contributed, "I came to the first but not to the one 10 years ago."

"So the rest of us are all newbies," Angie concluded. "We need to catch up. My turn first. I'm Angie Cadieux. I became a teacher and was once engaged to be married.

My fiancé and I were in a traffic accident, ending with us both in the hospital in critical condition. I survived, but he did not. To this day, I avoid a certain part of the 405 Freeway. Roughly 10 years ago, I got the calling and joined the Sisters of Temperance." She nudged Lori at her left and said, "You're next."

"I'm Lori Aames and used to be a real estate agent but gave up working to become a stay-at-home mom, homeschooling our twins." She added, "Now that they are in college, I'm toying with going back to work. We recently took over my parents' house in Seabreeze when they moved to Florida to retire."

Her husband winked at her and stated, "She became Lori Winter because she married me, Ray Winter. I started off as a computer science professor but quit teaching at UC San Diego when I was hired at Dercan as CIO in their IT department."

Gigi whispered, "What's a CIO?"

Dean rolled his eyes and muttered in her ear, "Chief Information Officer," while Heather already took her turn, saying, "You know me as Heather Jones, but I'm happily married to Jacob Levine, here," and she patted his hand. As for my profession, I'm a retail buyer for a major department store and Jacob is a nurse."

Heather's spouse looked even younger than his 36 years, which made Ray speak softly enough for only Lori to hear, "Is he old enough to have a glass of wine?"

"Don't be unkind," she whispered back.

Jacob was happy that he was not expected to comment, so Alex Kazarian took over, telling people that he owned a car wash business in Glendale and another in Eagle Rock. People around that table also learned that his wife, Michelle, was the cashier at the Glendale location.

Neither Raphael nor Lucia Torres went into details about their lives. He simply stated that he was a jockey and she was a dancer, teaching Latin dancing.

Dong Kim shared that he was a scientist, employed at the Jet Propulsion Laboratory in La Cañada Flintridge, working for NASA on robotic space exploration. His wife Chin Sun was a fellow scientist at JPL.

Martin Taylor said, "I'm Martin Taylor and the person to my left is my husband, Vito Taylor. We live in Escondido but travel a lot, since I'm a pianist and have engagements all over the US and beyond. Vito is a physical therapist, which is a blessing. He gives soothing massages when I'm stressed out."

Introductions had gone full circle around the table and Dean, seated at the other side of Angie, was last. He said, "I'm Dean Rickey, a programmer, and I live in Tucson, Arizona. I tried married life, but it's not for me. I'm a bit of a gambler; after all, life is but a gamble, right? I'm planning to relocate back to California soon, preferably to this area, if I can afford it. And please meet my friend Gigi."

Heather placed a hand in front of her mouth and muttered to Jacob, "He's still the same nerd, wearing a bow tie that makes him look like a clown."

Drinks and food was served, so conversations slowed to a minimum while the group concentrated on eating.

CHAPTER 4

With their palates satisfied, conversations started to flow with refills of wine and over dessert and coffee. With so many people in the large hall and folks chatting at each table, it got a bit loud.

Raising his glass, Dean shouted at Raphael across the table, "Here's to our famous jockey. And don't be shy. I've kept up with the racing industry. You *are* famous, no doubt. How about giving us some insider tips on the front runners?"

Not expecting an answer, he looked at Dong and said, "Hey there, *Gray Matter*, I see you're still as trim as ever. How do you find time to work out when you're busy firing rockets?" Dong did not credit him with a reply either, so he leaned over Angie and addressed Lori with, "Hail to the homecoming queen," raising his glass again.

To Ray, he said, "Hey there, Mr. Winter. You now work as CIO for Dercan. I'm impressed!" And he added, "You're the reason I became a programmer. Back when you were at UC San Diego, I was in your class when you taught computer programming for us kids at Seabreeze High. It was neat having a university professor on board, and you got me all fired up about the computer world."

"Correct. I was teaching the course as an experiment at your high school one semester, but sorry, I don't remember you," said Ray.

Gigi asked Dean, "What's Dercan?"

"You don't know? It's only the biggest high-tech company this side of the country," he hissed, and started to regret having hired her.

Then he looked beyond her and spoke to Martin, commenting, "You did not fit the norm back at school but sure have come a long way! I've never been to any of your concerts, but knowing a renowned artist like you may come in handy."

Glancing at Heather, Dean went on, "You were the wild party girl at Seabreeze High but seem to have turned respectable now. You must feel proud for having climbed the department store corporate ladder."

She darted an angry look at him as he addressed Alex Kazarian, saying, "So you own two car washes, congrats!"

As a final point he glanced at Angie and declared, "I'll try my best to behave, Your Grace."

His eyes then scanned them all as he remarked, "Looks like everyone at this table has a success story to tell and – –"

Alex had had enough of Dean and cut him short by talking about his car wash business with pride, pointing out that, unlike other car washes, his establishments did not use what he called "quicky machines" but washed all vehicles by hand. Then he glanced in Lori's direction and remarked, "Never mind Dean's mockery. You were a lovely and gracious homecoming queen and still are a beauty now."

"Well, thank you!" she said.

"And I remember Angie was part of your court."

Angie nodded in acknowledgment.

Michelle Kazarian became bored as classmates reminisced about Seabreeze High, with comments like, "Remember when Jillian jammed the lock in the bathroom and the janitor had to climb a ladder and let himself in through a window to rescue her? What a commotion!" And, "We about peed in our pants laughing when the math teacher sat on his reading glasses and crushed them to bits during a test." And, "Remember when somebody in the neighborhood let off firecrackers during an earthquake drill, and we all thought it was the real thing for a second?"

Martin remarked, "Those were gentler times when we only had earthquake and fire drills. Nowadays, schools deal with lockdowns all over the country because of mass killings, and parents worry whether their child will be alive at the end of the school day."

"You are so right," said Raphael. "The idea that someone could get murdered at school in our day was absurd."

"And yet, it happened!" Dean cried out.

"What the heck do you mean?"

"Remember Justin Picard?"

"That was suicide. He jumped from the turret. Everyone knew that," said an irate Heather.

"I beg to differ. He was pushed. I was a witness."

There was suddenly total silence at that table. Michelle, who had not paid much attention to their conversations before, was no longer bored and became alert.

Dong recovered first and asked, "So why didn't you speak up at the time?"

"I wasn't sure since I couldn't think of a motive and thought I might be mistaken. But now I figured out the motive and am sure."

"I think you're making it up," was Dong's response.

Dean's bombshell put a damper on the group and their conversations were forced for the rest of the evening.

As carefree laughter drifted over from another table, Lucia leaned toward Raphael and said, "I wish we'd chosen to sit with those people."

CHAPTER 5

Dean's accusation - - the group of people seated at his table took it as an accusation - - left a certain doom with all concerned.

On the hotel elevator ride up to their room, Chin Sun asked her husband, "Did you know this Justin Picard they were talking about?"

"Yes, but not well. He spent a great deal of time on the football field and did as little as possible academically."

"Did you like him?"

"No. He was a bully."

While walking along the corridor she inquired, "How did he bully you?"

"In our senior year he demanded that I write his essay."

"So he needed help with his writing. That doesn't sound like bullying to me," Chin Sun observed.

Dong stated, "He didn't ask for help or guidance and was not interested in contributing anything himself. He ordered me to write the entire essay."

"I see. And you refused?"

"Of course. And even any threat of beating me up didn't change my mind."

They had arrived at their room when she said, "Did he?"

"What?"

"Did he beat you up?"

"No, but I watched my back for the rest of the school year."

Later that night Chin Sun lay awake and realizing that Dong was not asleep either, she asked, "Do you believe that Dean told the truth about witnessing Justin's murder?"

"No. He made it up to look important. Justin committed suicide," Dong said with conviction.

On a lighter note his wife teased, "Sister Margaret, aka Angie, is very gracious. I'm not surprised that you took her to the senior prom." Then she nudged him and said, "So you were tagged as *Gray Matter.*"

"Could have been worse; people could've called me *Quark Matter.*"

CHAPTER 6

A few rooms away, the Kazarians had a hard time falling asleep too.

Michelle asked, "Do you believe Dean's accusation?"

"I don't know what to believe," Alex shot back. "Dean is such a weirdo that I wouldn't be surprised if he made it up. On the other hand, Justin Picard was not the type to take his own life, in my opinion."

"Did he leave a suicide note behind?"

"Not that I know of."

"What would have been his reason to take his own life?"

Alex recalled, "After he jumped, word got around that his home life had been miserable, as his parents went through a nasty divorce. He also had just received a rejection for a football scholarship at the university of his choice. I believe that was because his grade point average was below 2.3."

"Those don't sound like reasons to commit suicide," his wife said. And after a moment's reflection she asked, "Who would have had a motive to kill him?"

"I don't know. I wasn't his friend nor close to the people he hung out with. He had a lot of clout, being the school's top football player, but I was unimpressed since I was into soccer. I did know that he was a bully, though, and I can imagine that he made enemies."

"Well, let's not dwell on it and get some sleep."

CHAPTER 7

Raphael and Lucia Torres had been silent for the first couple of miles on their drive home.

Just before they reached their hometown of Del Mar, Lucia said, "It was the boy Justin who tormented you?"

"You've got that right," replied Raphael.

"Now I know what you meant by saying that there was no chance that he'd come to the reunion."

After a pause she said, "Tell me about him."

"There's not much to tell. He was *the* football star of Seabreeze High."

"Was anyone at our table tonight a close friend of his?"

"None of the guys that I know of, but Lori was his girlfriend."

"Interesting."

"Come to think of it, most guys had a crush on her, including me, but we knew better than to act on it, fearing what Justin would do to us."

There was more silence but as they drove up the driveway of their house, Lucia said, "When we stopped at the school on our way to the reunion, you stared up at that weird tower. Were you thinking of Justin?"

"Yes."

"Do you believe the man with the bow tie who claims that it was not suicide, but murder?"

"I don't know. Dammit."

CHAPTER 8

At around the same time, Heather and Jacob arrived at their home in San Diego. Jacob went straight to the bedroom, saying, "I have the morning shift tomorrow; I'd better get some shuteye."

"Sure, Hon. I hope you don't mind if I unwind for a bit," Heather replied, plopped herself on the recliner in the living room, and turned on the TV.

She could not concentrate on the TV program, though. Flashbacks from her high school days crept into her mind. She had tried hard to forget about them and had succeeded but now the past would not leave her alone, once more. Sure, the goody two-shoes homecoming queen was Justin's girlfriend, but he was screwing me, she thought, her anger coming over her again now, decades later. She remembered the day he jumped clearly. After their last period, they'd met on the turret - - known to some kids as *Lovers' Nest* - - as usual. But instead of getting down to business, she had picked a fight, giving him an ultimatum.

She was surprised that she remembered her shouted words after all this time: "I'm done with this, Justin. Either you drop Lori or you lose me. Your choice."

She remembered clearly having run down the steps leading up to the turret, not being able to shake the surprised look on his face. The next morning, as news about his jump went around school, she realized that she may have been the last person to see him alive.

CHAPTER 9

There was not much traffic on the I-15 Freeway heading North late at night, so Vito, at the wheel, had a relaxed drive home. But Martin was anything but relaxed.

He said, "We had such a lovely time and then Dean had to ruin it with his threat."

"You really think it was a threat?" Vito asked.

"What else could it be? The man practically accused one of us at that table of having killed Justin Picard."

"I've never met Dean before tonight, but in my opinion the man was out for shock effect."

"I don't understand what you mean."

"I might be wrong, but I think he's the type that craves attention. Look at the date he brought along! Ironically, nobody seemed to care about his young, sexy, companion, so he wanted to get noticed in a more outrageous way and made up the murder story about the boy who jumped off the tower."

Martin corrected, "It isn't a tower, only a turret."

"What's the difference?"

"A tower is a tall, standalone structure, while a turret is a smaller type of tower attached to a building."

In a British accent, Vito joked, "Tower, turret. Who bloody cares, my dear?"

As usual, he had a calming effect on his spouse. By the time they reached home, Martin was able to loosen up.

CHAPTER 10

Back in Seabreeze, the Winters were getting ready for bed. After brushing his teeth, Ray suddenly cried out, "Oh no!"

Lori stuck her head in the bathroom door and asked, "What's wrong?"

"I lost the wedding band."

"Again?" she exclaimed.

"Not to worry. I know where it is. It came off when washing my hands in the hotel bathroom, so I put it up on the mirror ledge. I bet it's still there. I'll go look for it first thing in the morning."

Later, lying next to each other, neither could sleep.

Ray said, "You didn't tell me about your plans of going back to work. Your mentioning it to the group was the first I heard of it."

Lori replied, "I've kept up my real estate license by renewing it regularly and now is the right time for me to go back to work. The agency offered me my job back."

"Are you sure that's what you want? Some kind of volunteer position would be less stressful."

When she did not answer, he brought up what was most on both of their minds and said, "I know that Dean's outburst about Justin's death stirred up painful memories for you, but let it go."

After a long pause, Lori replied, "I have a confession to make. Remember when we first met at the bleachers the day after Justin died?"

"How could I ever forget? You were sitting on the bottom bleacher, crying your head off, grieving over your boyfriend."

"That's just it. I wasn't bawling because of the loss, but rather out of guilt."

Ray took in a long breath but said nothing as she continued, "I broke up with him that very day. He waited for me as I came out of choir practice and said we needed to talk, leading me up to the turret when we were sure that the choir people had dispersed and wouldn't see us getting up the stairs. We'd been up there together a few times before, but I didn't like the place."

She remarked, "I'm sure you never went up to the turret, why would you? So you don't know what it looks like from inside. I never liked it. It was hard to breathe in the small space. Sure, there was a great view overlooking the town and the ocean beyond, but the spot was claustrophobic. There was a tiny table and bench, no windows, nothing but walls, except for the opening that led to a tiny balcony."

She continued with the account of her ordeal, saying, "When we got there, he started making out right away, and I knew that 'talk' was the furthest thing from his mind. We had gone through similar situations before and they always ended up with me telling him that I was not ready for sex. This time, though, he wouldn't take no for an answer and forced himself on me. I kicked him where it hurt, said I was breaking up with him, and then ran off."

She sat up in bed and stated, "So you see, I felt responsible for his suicide. Sure, he was down in the dumps over his parents' nasty divorce and not getting the scholarship he wanted, but I thought that my breaking up was the last straw."

Ray was speechless.

Lori lay back down and said, "I know this sounds heartless, but the possibility that Justin was pushed makes me feel better and not guilty any longer."

She was about to doze off as Ray said, "I have a confession of my own. I wanted you from the first time I saw you. Justin's jump or push - - whatever the case may be - - made it possible."

She yawned and remarked, "But during my high school days, you were my mentor, nothing more. We didn't date until I attended UC San Diego," Lori mumbled.

She was already drifted off to sleep when he remarked, "As you well know, I have tons of patience."

CHAPTER 11

At the convent of the Sisters of Temperance, Sister Margaret knelt beside her bed and said her nightly prayers. When she was done, she added, "Thank you, Lord, for a wonderful reunion, giving me a chance to bid my past farewell and now letting me fully concentrate on the future of teaching and helping the poor in foreign lands. And dear Jesus, forgive Dean Rickey for making up murder stories. I'm sure he just wanted some attention and meant no harm with his shocking fib. Amen."

She made the sign of the cross and then hopped into bed.

At the bed and breakfast, Dean's last thoughts before falling asleep were full of excitement. His bombshell had worked and prompted the reaction he'd anticipated. That was a genius idea he'd had to google everyone before coming to the reunion. And it sure was going to pay off. If he played his cards right, he would be able to move to Seabreeze. He had forgotten what a great small town it was until he toured it for the last couple days. The man was all fired up and could hardly wait until morning. Whereas Gigi, getting ready for bed at her place in San Diego, mused that, although her customer had been a bore and know-it-all, she at least got a nice meal out of the evening.

The person who had been targeted by Dean was also anticipating the next morning. They had been trying to forget about what happened to Justin Picard all those years ago and had almost succeeded. Now the sordid fact rushed back into mind and thanks to Dean would be revealed. The nerd needed to be stopped. The individual was a quick thinker and had formed a plan on the spur of the moment. If executed to perfection, life would continue as normal.

CHAPTER 12

Early Sunday morning, Dean was trekking west along the beach towards a small inlet, known as *The Cove*, situated close to the Del Mar border. He was barefoot, carrying his flip-flops and felt the cool sand dribbling between his toes with each step. The Cove was not an official name, but the town's inhabitants, and anyone who had ever lived in Seabreeze, knew its location. When the person had said, "Meet me at The Cove at eight o'clock tomorrow morning," Dean had easily remembered the little spot carved out by the ocean.

He got to the place first. Like expected, it was deserted at that early hour on a chilly September morning. Except for seagulls circling above, he had not encountered a soul since walking along the beach. The Cove was ideal for their rendezvous; it gave them privacy, yet was in the open.

Dean saw the person approaching and was determined to stay steadfast with his demand. He knew that he held the winning card in this game. The request about a regular tie, not a bow tie, was a bit strange, but he had packed one in case he needed to wear it for a job interview while in Southern California.

Checking his watch, Dean said, "Hello there! You're right on time."

Not interested in small talk, the other shot back, "Let's get this over with. You do know that blackmail is a crime, right?"

Dean replied, "Murder is a much worse crime and there is no statute of limitations. And he added, "Anyway, I'm not asking for money, so don't consider it blackmail."

"It *is* blackmail and you know it. So tell me where you were when you claim to have seen me pushing Justin off the turret."

"I actually did not see you push him, but I saw you come down from the turret. I forgot my homework and came back to get it from my locker after school hours. On my way out, I clearly saw you rushing from the entry leading up to the turret. Later, when the news got around about Justin, I put two and two together. You had no business being up at that turret."

"Why didn't you come forward at the time?"

"As I said at the reunion, it took me all those years to figure out the motive, but figure it out I did," replied Dean.

"Tell me the motive."

The former did as ordered and the other person hesitated for a second about going ahead with the plan. Although Dean spoke the truth, it sounded far-fetched. Still, a jury might believe Dean, so the person could not take that chance.

The individual said, "Before we go into details about how to proceed, did you remember to bring a tie?"

"Yes, and I've been practicing," Dean said with a smirk.

"Let's see."

Dean let the flip-flops fall to the sand, retrieved the necktie from his pocket, slung it around his neck, and was about to tie it at the throat.

"No, no, you're doing it wrong!" And in a flash, his assailant's surgical gloved hands came out of hiding from their jacket pockets, grabbed both ends of the tie, pulled them tight, and squeezed.

A short struggle took place, but Dean had been taken by total surprise, and when he tried to free himself of the hold around his neck, the tie was pulled even firmer. It was over in a few moments. His airway was blocked so that he could no longer breathe.

As he lost consciousness, the killer let the lifeless body fall backward to the sandy ground, keeping a firm grip, then double-knotted the tie before finally letting go. Looking in all directions, making sure that they were still alone as far as the eye could see, the culprit stayed by the victim for another minute to make certain that Dean was dead. It took a great effort to stick it out for an entire minute.

With the deed accomplished, the murderer turned around and then walked along the shore, without a glance back.

Half an hour later a jogger happened upon the ghastly scene.

CHAPTER 13

The town of Seabreeze was too small to maintain its own police department and had contracted law enforcement services from the San Diego County Sheriff's Department. Detective Thomas Scharfkopf, of said department, was not pleased when he got the call about having to investigate a homicide at Seabreeze's beach on Sunday morning, September 8. When the summons came, he was at the golf course, waiting for a tee time. He told his two buddies that he was sorry but a threesome was not to be, and rushed off.

Those who knew Detective Scharfkopf well, and understood a bit of German, thought his name suited him. He had a "sharp head" indeed. He also had a lot of experience under his belt, was past middle age, and looked forward to retiring at the end of the year.

The coroner and the detective arrived simultaneously at the crime scene, where the team had already cordoned off the area. The detective checked the time. It was 9:02 a.m. The two men carefully stepped over the yellow tape and took a close look.

What they saw was the body of a man in his mid to late forties wearing sweatpants and a windbreaker. He was barefoot. A pair of flip-flops lay by his side. He had obviously been strangled with a necktie. The corpse's face wore a panicked expression, and his tongue hung out of his mouth.

While the coroner performed a brief preliminary examination of the corpse, Scharfkopf talked to the jogger who was detained nearby. The young man was shaken but gave a coherent account. A resident of Seabreeze, he had gone for his morning jog along the beach, which was his habit. When he'd come around the bend toward The Cove, he saw a person lying in the sand, which was strange, early in the morning on a gloomy day. Coming closer, the young man realized there had been something weird about the person's posture, so he had changed to a sprint, thinking the person may be ill and needed help.

At this point of his narrative, the young man glanced over to what was happening beyond the yellow tape and became agitated as he visualized the corpse he'd happened upon.

Detective Scharfkopf said, "What you found was not pleasant. So you can skip what you saw. I need to know whether you touched the body."

"I did not! It was obvious that the man was beyond help. I already told this to another officer."

"Good," said the detective. "Did you encounter anyone before you arrived at the scene?"

"No, not a single person."

"Did you happen to look at the time when you got here?"

"Yes, sir. It was 8:30 and I called 911 right away. Can I go home now?"

"Just one more question. Do you know the person you found strangled?"

"No, sir, he's a stranger."

Scharfkopf asked for his name, address, and phone number, and then released him.

Meanwhile, the coroner had done his job, the photographer had also done his, and the tie had been dropped into an evidence bag. A wallet was found on the victim's person with a driver's license identifying him as Dean Rickey, residing in Tucson, Arizona. Also tucked away in his wallet was a business card from a local bed and breakfast place. The only other object retrieved from the victim's pocket was his cell phone.

"Can you give me an approximate time of death?" The detective asked.

"Very recent. According to his body temperature, I'd say between 8:00 and 8:30," replied the coroner.

"There are no visible footprints in the sand, except ours."

"You've got that right. The victim and the perpetrator were obviously barefoot and so was the witness. They barely left a track."

As the coroner was getting ready to leave with his charge, he joked, "You learn something new every day!"

"What's that?" the detective asked.

"In all my years as a medical examiner, I've never come across a tie being the murder weapon." And on a serious note he added, "We'll examine it for DNA. As for the rest, I'll let you know when my final report is ready," and he followed the corpse bag, which was in the process of being hauled into his vehicle.

There was nothing left to do at the scene for Detective Scharfkopf, and he trekked off the beach toward where his car was parked.

CHAPTER 14

On Monday morning Detective Scharfkopf was on his way to the convent of the Sisters of Temperance in San Diego. The day before, he had gone straight from the crime scene to the bed and breakfast, making use of the card he'd found in Dean's wallet. A woman ran the place and she had been cooperative. She acknowledged that Dean Rickey was one of her lodgers. When asked if she knew Dean's purpose for staying in town, she had been helpful. According to her, the gentleman had stayed there since Friday and had booked the place for an entire week.

He had told her that he was combining a class reunion on Saturday with a bit of vacation by the beach. He had also remarked that he may be relocating to the general area of Seabreeze in the near future. When asked if she knew where the reunion had taken place, she said that Dean had mentioned the resort hotel by the ocean.

"What about this morning?" the detective had inquired. "Did you see your lodger leave?"

"Sure," she had replied, "He took off right after the early breakfast. We usually serve breakfast at two different times to make it convenient for our guests."

When the detective probed if he was wearing a tie, she seemed surprised and asked, "A tie? He was wearing no tie. As far as I know, he was headed for the beach."

He then wanted to see the room Dean had occupied. Dress pants and jacket were hanging in the wardrobe. The rest of his clothes and belongings were stashed in a small suitcase, sitting on a luggage stand. He told the lady that someone from his team would come to collect the things shortly, and to please lock the room in the meantime. He had handed her a business card, in case she remembered something else about Dean.

Procedure had made him order a background check on the victim, since 'next of kin' was not identifiable from his belongings.

Next, he had paid the hotel a visit, where he learned that the organizer and financier of the elaborate reunion had been a nun. A nun! This case got stranger by the minute.

The detective rehashed all this in his mind while driving to the convent. Once there, he showed his credentials to the nun at the gate, then was directed to the Mother Superior's parlor, which was comparable to a small studio, sparsely furnished with a modest coffee table and three easy chairs. Through an open doorway he got a peek into the Mother Superior's office, consisting of a desk, an office chair, and a couple of file cabinets.

Detective Scharfkopf sat waiting in the parlor, glancing at his watch. It had been ten minutes since he'd been ushered in, and as he was wondering if the nuns had forgotten about him, Mother Superior sailed in, and he got to his feet.

There was something majestic about the old lady, who was in her eighties, yet the detective was sure she ruled with an iron fist.

"Sorry to have kept you waiting, Officer - - " she looked at him questioningly.

"Scharfkopf, and I'm a detective."

" - - Detective Scharfkopf. We had adoration in the chapel and I could not get away. I understand you wish to talk to Sister Margaret in your official capacity."

He did not know how to address her and said, "Yes, ma'am."

"May I ask what about?"

"Are you aware that Sister Margaret attended her class reunion on Saturday?"

"Yes, sir. I know all about my sisters."

"I am investigating the homicide of a classmate who attended the event."

There was a slight intake of her breath before she said, "God save his or her soul."

He stated, "I wish to talk with Sister Margaret alone."

To which she replied, "If you are planning to interrogate her, I need to be present."

"Nothing as alarming as that. I understand the sister had organized the reunion, so I need to get names and addresses from her, as well as maybe some insight, if she has any."

"I see. I will inform Sister Margaret of what you need. Have a seat," she ordered and sailed out of her parlor again.

He almost saluted but said instead, "Thank you, ma'am."

CHAPTER 15

Detective Scharfkopf had expected Sister Margaret to come with a yellow notepad or a manila folder at best. He was in for a surprise when she appeared with a tablet. The Sisters of Temperance kept up with the times, he mused.

Before the detective could start the interview, Sister Margaret took the initiative and said, "Mother Superior informed me that you are conducting an investigation. What is it about?"

"Dean Rickey's homicide, to be blunt," he replied.

"So I was wrong," she murmured. Then she crossed herself and said, "God rest his soul!" and closed her eyes in a moment of prayer. Opening them seconds later, she asked, "When and how was he killed?"

"He was strangled yesterday morning."

She said softly, almost to herself, "How fast things change. When I saw him Saturday, he seemed to have not a worry in the world."

"Yes, Sister, tell me about Saturday. I understand that you organized and financed your 30-year high school class reunion."

"Right. Mother Superior said you needed names and phone numbers of my former classmates."

"Correct, but let's talk a bit first. I am curious, what motivated you to be in charge of the reunion, and how did you have the means to finance the big event? I talked with the hotel people and know what an elaborate gathering it was."

She took a moment before she replied, almost as if she had to search for an answer. Then she explained, "The financing part is easy; I inherited a large amount of money. As for motivation, I am scheduled to depart at the end of the month to serve in our foreign missions. Most likely, I will never return to my homeland. Call it nostalgia, or ending the chapter of my past, if you want."

"Fair enough. Now tell me, was there assigned seating?"

"No. People sat wherever they wanted at round tables, seating 15 people each."

"Do you know with whom Dean Rickey shared a table?"

She smiled and stated, "He sat at mine."

"That makes it easy, then. Name the folks who sat with you."

Sister Margaret pictured the round table in her mind's eye and gave an account of everyone in order of their seating, saying, "My best friend, Lori, sat to my left, followed by her husband, Ray. Next to him sat Heather with hubby Jacob. Then came Alex with Michelle, then Raphael with wife Lucia, followed by Dong and Chin Sun. To their left was Martin with husband Vito. And sitting right next to me to my right was Dean and his date, Gigi."

"I'm glad you've got a good memory," the detective commented. "You said someone named Lori was your best friend. I take it that you also know some of the others who sat at your table?"

"They were all former classmates I knew back in our school days - - some of them not well - - but except for Ray, I had met none of their spouses before Saturday."

The detective probed, "When I first told you about Dean Rickey, you said under your breath that you were wrong. What did you mean by that?"

Sister Margaret was hesitant with her reply, debating how much information she was going to divulge to the law enforcer. Being a good citizen won, and she told it all. Her statement could no longer hurt poor Dean, she decided. She related the entire after-dinner conversations, instigated by Dean, ending with his final bombshell about Justin Picard.

Detective Scharfkopf paid keen attention to her narrative and then said, "Explain the turret. I mean, what was a turret doing on a school campus?"

"Oh, it was a weird extra structure towering over the centralized two-story building. I have no idea what its function was. Kids called it *Lovers' Nest*. I never went up to the turret myself, but I once saw an artwork from a student who went there to draw. Remembering that drawing, I know that the view from the turret overlooking the town and the ocean is spectacular."

Then he asked, "So Dean Rickey was accusing someone present at that table of being a murderer. Was he specific?"

"No. He only said that he'd been a witness."

"I'm getting the picture." And he inquired, "How well did you know Justin Picard?"

"Not well. I had no classes with him, but Lori was his girlfriend, so I learned stuff about him through her."

"What kind of stuff?"

"Nothing earthshaking, just that he had an unhappy home life and in his senior year did not get the football scholarship he applied for because of his low GPA."

The detective remarked, "I can imagine you did some double dating with the couple and the boy you were going out with."

"No, we did not. I always had the feeling that Justin resented me. He didn't want to share Lori with anyone. He wanted to keep her all to himself."

"I see. He was controlling?"

"He tried, but Lori is a free spirit and can't be controlled."

"Thanks for the detailed account, but you have not answered my question about your remark of 'being wrong.'"

She sighed and replied, "At the time I thought that Dean made the whole thing up - - about Justin Picard not having committed suicide - - to make himself feel important. Now I realize that I was wrong. Someone in our group must have felt threatened." She shuddered, adding, "This is upsetting."

The detective was afraid she might burst into tears and quickly said, "I think we are about done. Please give me people's addresses and phone numbers. I'm only interested in your former classmates; no need to give me their spouses info."

She scrolled to the required data on her tablet and texted it to his phone. He glanced at the addresses and said, "So two people live out of our area. One resides in Glendale, the other in La Cañada Flintridge. They had a long drive home."

"Correct, but both parties stayed at the hotel in Seabreeze where the reunion was held. I believe that Dong and his wife are making a vacation out of it and are still there."

The basics accomplished, Scharfkopf was almost embarrassed as he said, "Just for the record, where were you yesterday morning, September 8, from 8:00 a.m. until 8:30 a.m.?"

"At Sunday mass, which starts at eight o'clock," she replied.

"Can anyone confirm that?"

"I went with two other sisters," and she gave him their names.

Even more ill at ease, the detective continued, "Everyone who sat at that table is a person of interest. Theoretically speaking, I have to advise you not to leave the country in the near future."

"Theoretically speaking," she shot back, "I'm leaving for my mission at the end of the month. If you have a problem with that, I suggest you take it up with Mother Superior."

He could not prevent a grin and got up to leave, saying, "Thank you for your cooperation. I appreciate it."

When he was at the door, she asked, "Is it possible that Dean's perpetrator is an outsider? I mean, someone from Arizona could have followed him here."

"Nothing is impossible," he replied.

While driving away from the convent Detective Scharfkopf thought, looks like the victim was a blackmailer and it is up to me to figure out who he blackmailed. It was also obvious to him that he needed to know what went on at that high school three decades ago in order to solve the current case.

Sister Margaret, for her part, kneeled in one of the chapel's pews and prayed for Dean's soul, as well as the killer's.

CHAPTER 16

Detective Scharfkopf chose to interview Dong next, while the Kims were still in the neighborhood, but first he swung by the County Sheriff's Department and gave the list of persons of interest to a team member with the order to obtain their business addresses. After all, he assumed that most would be at work. He also asked his subordinate to begin an investigation into Justin Picard's death of 30 years ago.

The news about Dean Rickey was broadcast that morning and appeared in the local paper. A murder in the peaceful small town of Seabreeze shook people to the core.

Dong and Chin Sun were about ready for their short drive to San Diego to visit the USS Midway Museum and the San Diego Museum of Art, among other attractions, when the detective knocked at their hotel door.

He showed his credentials and asked for a few minutes of Dong's time.

Dong switched off the TV and said, "Is this about Dean? We just heard the shocking news."

"Correct. I'm interviewing his former classmates who sat at his table during Saturday's reunion." And he added, "So you were shocked?"

"Sure. We've never known anyone who ended up murdered before."

"Is there a place I can interview you in private?" Detective Scharfkopf asked.

Chin Sun was about to disappear into the bathroom but Dong held her back, saying, "Stay," and to the detective, "I have no secrets from my wife."

The small sitting area in the room held only two chairs, so Chin Sun sat down on the edge of the unmade king size bed and said, "Pretend I'm not here."

The detective continued, "The reason Dean Rickey's homicide should not come as a big surprise is the accusation he made during the course of the previous evening."

Dong smiled and said, "You've talked to Angie, which makes sense. How else could you have obtained my name and whereabouts?"

"Who is Angie?"

"She's Sister Margaret now, but I still think of her as Angie. To answer your question, I did not take Dean's accusation seriously and didn't think for a minute that Justin Picard was pushed from the turret."

"What do you think now?"

"Obviously someone silenced Dean because he must have spoken the truth."

Scharfkopf said, "Put your mind back to 30 years ago. How well did you know the boy that fell to his death?"

"Not well. We had nothing in common. He was the number one football player of the school. As for me, kids nicknamed me *Grey Matter*. That should put you in the picture."

"It does," the detective said with a grin. "What was your knowledge about Justin Picard's fall at the time?"

"That he committed suicide because of trouble in his home life, and the fact that he didn't get the football scholarship he'd applied for."

The detective scratched his head and pressed further, "Did that explanation sound plausible to you?"

"I didn't think much about it, to tell the truth," said Dong.

"Let's get back to the present. "Where were you Sunday morning, September 8, from 8:00 a.m. until 8:30 a.m.?"

Dong stated, "Right here at the hotel. Oh wait! I was gone for a short time and walked to a rental place nearby, checking out snorkeling equipment. We are planning to go snorkeling this week and I wanted to make sure we can rent everything we'll need." He turned his head toward Chin Sun and asked, "When was that?"

She stated, "I wasn't ready to leave the room yet but checked the time. You left shortly before eight."

"And I was back in a flash," he said.

The detective inquired, "Where is the rental place?"

"Along the beachfront, not even half a block east from here."

"You work at JPL in La Cañada Flintridge, correct?"

"Yes, sir. And so does my wife."

That concluded the interview and, on his way out the door, Detective Scharfkopf instructed Dong to keep himself available for further questioning and not to leave the country anytime soon.

Left to themselves, Chin Sun remarked, "I didn't like all those questions the detective tossed your way. Think he suspects you as the killer?"

"He has to consider everyone; that's his job," Dong replied.

CHAPTER 17

Minutes later, the Kims started on their short drive to San Diego. Dong entered the USS Midway Museum's address of 910 N. Harbor Dr. into his GPS and said, "Since we're getting a late start we might as well stop to eat lunch first. The museum is alongside Navy Pier, where there are plenty of restaurants to choose from."

"Good, I'm getting hungry," Chin Sun agreed.

He continued, "Funny, when we lived in Seabreeze, our family never visited any San Diego tourist attractions. My folks were too busy making ends meet, and I was expected to put all my energy into studying and getting straight A's. I'm looking forward to exploring the USS Midway and have read up about it. I learned that it was the longest serving aircraft carrier of the 20th century. It is also known as having carried out humanitarian missions."

He was on a roll and went on, "On every anniversary of the September 11 attacks in 2001, the museum holds a memorial service in remembrance of the lives lost during the catastrophe. That's this Wednesday, but I'm sure the place will be crowded, so we're better off going today."

Chin Sun had only listened halfheartedly to his history lesson, her mind having drifted to the interview with the law enforcer. She suddenly said, "I wonder if it was wise for you to admit that you went away for a few minutes to check out the rental place during the time the detective mentioned."

"I have nothing to hide," Dong shot back. "Besides, the police have a way of finding out about these things on their own, so it's best to tell the truth."

"You didn't tell him about the threats the bully made, though."

"What threats? Oh, you're talking about Justin Picard and his threats to beat me up if I didn't write his essay."

"Exactly. Why didn't you tell him?"

"That was 30 years ago! The detective has no way of checking up on it."

They had arrived at the outskirts of San Diego and tried to put Detective Scharfkopf and his agenda out of their minds.

CHAPTER 18

Scharfkopf also drove back to San Diego and ate his "to go" sandwich at his desk. He had a minuscule office, barely accommodating a desk, chair, and file cabinet. Still, he was happy to have a door he could shut, keeping the noise from the rest of the Sheriff's Department out.

Paperwork relating to other cases in progress were piling up at his desk, concerning crimes like burglaries, possession of illegal drugs, and domestic violence. The solving of a homicide, though, took priority.

He learned two new facts on that Monday afternoon about Dean Rickey's case. An officer on his team informed him that the victim's phone did not register any incoming or outgoing calls on Saturday night or Sunday morning. The officer also handed him a business card from an escort service that he had found tucked away in the pocket of the dress jacket that had been among the victim's personal belongings retrieved from the bed and breakfast place.

Interesting, thought Detective Scharfkopf. How did the killer arrange for a meeting with the victim without any phone contact? The two must have made arrangements right then and there at the reunion. That could not have happened at the dinner table with all other people as witnesses. No matter how it was done, the killer was smart not to use phone contact, I give him or her that.

He wondered, an escort service? The victim's date, Fru-Fru, or Lulu - - no, he believed it was Gigi - - may have been a girlfriend for hire.

And he mused about a different matter. He was positive that the killer brought the tie, either by wearing it or keeping it handy. That the victim, wearing sweatpants and a windbreaker, was not dressed in a tie stands to reason. But he needed to wait for the DNA results found on the tie to be 100% sure.

The detective's mind switched to the interview with Dong Kim. The one thing he had learned from the man was that he'd had nothing in common with Justin Picard. Other than that, nothing surfaced that he hadn't already learned from Sister Margaret. A motive for killing the boy would be hard to figure out 30 years later, not only for the two suspects he'd talked to today but for all others yet to be questioned.

As for an alibi, according to his wife, Dong had left the hotel before eight on Sunday morning to check on snorkeling equipment and stated to have been 'back in a flash.' That statement prompted the detective to stop by the rental place on his drive out of Seabreeze. The clerk behind the counter confirmed that Dong had been by to inquire about equipment on Sunday and was positive about the time. Dong had been waiting at the door when the place opened at 8:00 a.m.

Scharfkopf deduced that after leaving the rental shop, Dong could have turned around, bypassed the hotel, and kept walking west along the waterfront until reaching The Cove. It was a stretch, but could be done in about 15 minutes, if walked briskly. The jogger had happened upon the homicide at 8:30 and had not seen a soul on his way. The killer - - whether it was Dong or someone else - - could have returned to where he came from by an inland route.

He made notes of all that he had learned so far in the Dean Rickey case. That accomplished, his mind drifted away from the job, and he pondered the traveling he and his wife were planning after his retirement at the end of the year.

CHAPTER 19

Heather Jones-Levine had a demanding job as a retail buyer. Her office was on the third floor of a major department store building in San Diego. She continually looked for new products to be sold at her store to ensure her company's competitiveness with other retailers. She had to identify customer preferences and forecast consumer trends. Evaluating supplier options according to prices and quality, then determining the best choices, was not easy.

On the other hand, she was great at negotiating terms of agreements to achieve the best deal for her company. What she enjoyed most about her job was attending events, fairs, and exhibitions to remain competitive with market trends.

She was especially busy on Tuesday morning, September 10, when Detective Scharfkopf came to interview her. Her phone was on speaker while she rummaged on what the detective perceived as chaos on her desk. Miraculously, there was order in her disarray, and she found the sample product she was looking for at first try, while simultaneously motioning him to the chair across her desk with her free hand.

When she was off the phone, he said, "I see you're busy. I'll be brief. I'm Detective Scharfkopf and - -"

She interrupted, "September is always busy with getting a handle on Christmas," then continued, "I heard about Dean's murder, so I was expecting you, Detective."

"I'll get straight to the point," he said. "How well did you know Dean Rickey?"

"I had a couple of classes with him but didn't really know him. He was a nerd, and still is - - I mean was."

"Sister Margaret shared the comments he made at your table during the reunion dinner. He was not exactly kind to you when mentioning your high school days."

"That's right. He said I'd been a party girl."

"Were you?"

She laughed and admitted, "Hell, yes. But then I grew up."

The detective cracked a smile too and said, "Thanks for being honest."

"You would have found out anyway when talking to other classmates."

"What did you make of his claim that he'd been a witness to a murder?"

"At the time I thought he was lying, in a stupid attempt to make himself look important. Now it's obvious that he told the truth."

Scharfkopf inquired, "How well did you know Justin Picard?"

Heather had been afraid of that question from the second that he had stepped into her office. Her first instinct was to answer 'not well' but she changed her mind. There was a chance that others had known about her relationship with Justin and may blab it to the detective.

She admitted, "We were an item in our senior year."

"According to Sister Margaret, Lori was his girlfriend."

Heather tried to keep the bite out of her voice when she replied, "Sure, but she wasn't a party girl."

"I see. He played the field, not only where football was concerned."

The phone rang but Heather ignored it and let it go to voicemail, saying, "You've got that right. As a matter of fact, I met him up at the turret after school hours the day he was killed. When I heard the news about his jumping off the turret, I thought that I must have been the last person to see him alive. Now I know differently. The killer had that privilege. Justin was alive and well when I left him."

The phone rang again and she put the person on hold and said, "Are we about done?"

"Just a couple more questions. At the reunion, did you notice people leaving the room."

"Sure, most of us had to use the restrooms, which were not in the hall. You had to go out the door to the lobby. And of course, folks had to go all the way out of the building to smoke."

At last the detective asked the crucial question, "Where were you Sunday morning, September 8, from 8:00 a.m. until 8:30 a.m.?"

"Asleep in bed," she stated.

"Can anyone verify that?"

"Nope. My husband was long gone for his morning shift. You just have to take my word for it."

She waved him good-bye while pressing the button to talk with the person she had put on hold.

On the elevator down to the ground floor, Detective Scharfkopf thought, that woman is an interesting person. I could see the wheels turning in her mind when she hesitated to let me know about her relationship with the boy who fell to his death. One little puzzle of the investigation was solved in his mind now. The killer and the blackmailer arranged to meet at The Cove when either using the restroom or going outdoors to smoke.

CHAPTER 20

The Winters' residence was in walking distance from Seabreeze High School in what was now an affluent neighborhood. Detective Scharfkopf did not know much about architecture, but he identified their home as Spanish Revival with its stucco walls and terracotta roof.

He came unannounced and found Lori home on Tuesday afternoon. When ringing the doorbell, he heard barking coming from inside. She opened the door a crack and he introduced himself by showing his credentials. She ordered, "Hush Duke!" to the schnauzer at her feet and ushered Scharfkopf inside.

Appreciating the domed ceiling of the entryway he followed her to the den, where she ordered Duke to his bed in the corner of the room. The schnauzer let loose one last bark, then obeyed. She motioned the detective into a comfortable chair and offered him a beverage. He declined, so she sat down on the loveseat, facing him.

He was aware of something gripping about her. She was pretty, but that was not the essence. He sat across from one of those rare women whose beauty went beyond skin-deep and lasted a lifetime.

He remarked, "You have a charming home."

"Thanks, it's comfortable. We were lucky to take it over from my parents when they moved to Florida."

"I'm fortunate to find you home. You must be working remotely."

She said, "I've been a stay-at-home mom for a long time, but now that our twin girls went off to college last month, I'm ready to become a career woman again." She smiled and added, "I'm trying to convince my husband that it's the right thing to do."

"What is your profession?"

"I'm a real estate agent."

Enough of the pleasantries, the detective decided and said, "I'm sure you've learned of Dean Rickey's homicide."

She nodded.

"I'm interviewing all of Dean's classmates who sat at his table during your high school reunion."

She nodded again.

"Sister Margaret filled me in on conversations held at that table during the event, in particular, the topics that Dean brought up."

Lori stated, "Typical of him, he made silly remarks to most of us throughout the evening, but his bombshell toward the end made everyone uneasy."

"So you knew him well?"

"In high school, fairly well. I had some classes with him. We never met afterwards. Last Saturday was the first time we had seen each other in 30 years."

"What did you think of him back in your school days?"

She took her time with answering, then said, "I felt sorry for him. He was known as a nerd and was basically a loner. He liked computers but was awkward with kids and made strange comments."

"What about at the reunion?" he asked.

"He hadn't changed much," she replied.

Detective Scharfkopf continued, "Let's get to Justin Picard. How well did you know him?"

She smirked and said, "I have the feeling that you already know that he was my boyfriend."

"Correct. I also know that he was the football star of Seabreeze High. What position did he play?"

"Quarterback," she replied.

"What was your opinion about Dean Rickey's claim that Justin did not jump from the turret but was pushed?"

Her answer did not come right away. The detective started to think that she was not going to comment when she said, "It was a relief."

"How so?"

Again, she hesitated but after a long moment confessed, "I felt guilty. You see, I had broken up with him that very day and thought that it might have contributed to his committing suicide."

It was evident that she regretted having revealed as much, as she broke out in a nervous little cough. The schnauzer picked up on it, raised his head out of the dog bed, and growled.

"It's alright, Duke," she said, and he lay back down.

Scharfkopf asked, "When and where was that?"

"It was after school hours. I had come out of choir practice and found Justin waiting for me. We went up to the turret to talk."

"I see. Did you come down together?"

"No, I left in a hurry, but he stayed up there. The next day, when I heard about his jumping, I thought he must have done so soon afterwards, and that I had been the last person to see him alive."

After another pause, she added, "Now we know that the killer was that last person."

"Do you know who found him?"

"The custodian did. Living close to the school, I heard sirens that evening but had no idea it was the paramedics coming for Justin."

The detective said, "Let's get back to the present. Where were you Sunday morning, September 8, from 8:00 a.m. until 8:30 a.m.?"

"Oh, was that when poor Dean was strangled?" Not waiting for an answer she continued, "I was walking Duke around our neighborhood at that time, like I do every morning."

"Can anyone verify that?"

"Not really. Ray, my husband, went back to the hotel. I might have seen other people out for an early walk, but didn't pay attention. My main focus was on Duke and to clean up after he did his business."

Scharfkopf said, "Speaking of your husband, that reminds me. In general, I'm only interested in interviewing people who went to school with Dean Rickey, not their spouses. But in your husband's case, I understand that he was teaching at Seabreeze High School. Strictly speaking, he is also a person of interest, so I'd like a word with him too. I assume that I can find him at work most days?"

"Sure. He works for Dercan."

"Dercan in Irvine?"

"Yes. Do you want the address?"

"No need. I know the place."

The detective asked one last thing. "Do you happen to know who is a smoker among the people who sat at your table?"

"Dean was. I smelled it on his clothing."

"Anyone else you can think of?"

"No, sorry."

He got up to leave and instructed the lady to keep herself available for further questioning, if necessary. Duke jumped out of his bed and joined his mistress to escort him to the front door.

As the detective drove away, he thought, two suspects told me that they initially believed they had been the last person to see Justin alive. Interesting.

Lori for her part thought, I shouldn't have told him that I'd broken up with Justin and certainly not that I was up at the turret with him that day.

Aloud she asked, "What do you think, Duke?" and got a couple of barks back for an answer.

CHAPTER 21

The last horse races for the season at the Del Mar track had been on Sunday, September 8. There would be a lull now until Raphael Torres would race again at Santa Anita Park in October.

As a favor to both his agent and the owner of the horse, Raphael was training Prancer at San Luis Rey Downs. Early Wednesday morning on September 11, he had driven to the horse training facility, located a 25-minute drive inland from his hometown of Del Mar. Prancer had great potential and Raphael was going to ride him next month at Santa Anita. He didn't get paid for the morning's workout, but it couldn't hurt to get familiar with Prancer. Besides, Raphael was happiest when he was on a horse.

He had become a jockey soon after high school and could have never imagined another life. Thanks to finding a top-notch agent, he'd moved up in the ranks of jockeys, ending up as an elite rider. In addition to the fee for each mount, jockeys earned 10% of the winning purse. Consequently, Raphael had been able to make a good living and even garnered a sizable nest egg.

The notable jockey had been extremely lucky to have had few serious injuries, considering the many times he had been thrown off a horse. A dislocated shoulder, a broken ankle, a couple of concussions, and lots of scrapes and bruises was the extent of it.

Sadly, horse racing was no longer what it had been three decades ago. In those days, race tracks were open five to six days a week, compared with two or three now. Spectator crowds were ten times as big then. With all the off-track betting, people no longer needed to be present to place their wagers. One good thing, though; the job was now safer for the jockeys. 30 years ago, they wore no flack vests. Now a body protector vest was mandatory, even when training.

Raphael would be ready to retire in a couple of years and planned to take on some other position within the racing industry, like becoming a trainer or patrol judge, which might later lead to steward. His wife, Lucia, wanted him to help her start her own dancing studio, but it was hard to picture his life without horses.

At the moment, he had finished up the 1 ½ -mile gallop with Prancer, hoisted himself out of the saddle, and handed Prancer to the hot-walker, who held onto him while the groom hosed him off and gave him water to drink. Then the hot-walker sauntered the horse for 30 minutes before returning him to the stables.

As Raphael walked by the trainer's office on his way out of the place, the trainer motioned him inside and said, "You have someone waiting for you."

Detective Scharfkopf introduced himself to Raphael, and the trainer took the hint, saying, "I'm needed on the course," and went out the door.

Alone in the office, the two men seated themselves in the small waiting area and Scharfkopf said, "I've watched you galloping that beauty of a horse from a distance and I'm impressed. It's as if rider and horse became one."

"That's as it should be," Raphael replied.

"It makes your job look easy, but I know that's far from the case." And he came to the point, adding, "My work isn't easy either. I bet you know why I'm here to see you."

"You're investigating Dean Rickey's murder."

"Correct. Tell me about him."

"We had one class together back in high school, but I hardly knew him then, let alone now. Haven't seen the guy in decades. He was a stranger to me last Saturday at the class reunion."

When prompted, Raphael went into detail about the conversations at his table during the event, but the detective learned nothing new that other suspects had not already told him.

Then he said, "Let's talk about Justin Picard."

"I tried to avoid him. He was bad news," said Raphael, without hesitation.

"I've heard that he was a celebrated quarterback at Seabreeze High."

"That's right, but he was a mean SOB and always made sure he was surrounded by his cronies when tormenting kids. I don't know what Lori saw in him."

"I believe Lori Winter was his girlfriend."

"That's right, but she was Lori Aames then."

"You liked her?"

Raphael grinned and admitted, "I had a crush on her. Most guys did, but she was also well-liked by girls."

Scharfkopf said, "Now put your mind back to the present. Where were you Sunday morning, September 8, from 8:00 a.m. until 8:30 a.m.?"

"My alarm went off at eight o'clock, so I was home, eating breakfast and then showering. I had my last race of the season at Del Mar, and I needed to get to work one hour before my first mount, which was at 1:00 p.m. I like to get there much earlier, though. It only takes me 15 minutes to drive from my house over to the tracks, but I don't like to rush before my races."

"When did you leave to go to work?"

"At a quarter past eleven."

"And before that? Did you leave your house at any time?"

"No, sir."

"Can anyone confirm that?"

"Sure. Lucia, my wife, was home all morning."

That concluded the interview. Detective Scharfkopf thanked him for his time, ordered him not to leave the country, and walked back to where his car was parked.

As Raphael walked out the office door, he almost collided with the trainer, who was coming back inside. The trainer looked at him and asked, "Are you in trouble with the law?"

"Not at all," replied Raphael. "The detective is investigating a case that has nothing to do with me. I'm sorry that I couldn't help him."

"Good to know," said the trainer.

CHAPTER 22

On that Wednesday afternoon Detective Scharfkopf sat in his office at the San Diego County Sheriff's Department, reading the coroner's autopsy report of Dean Rickey, which had landed on his desk. He read it a second time to make sure he had not missed anything important.

Skipping the medical jargon, it came down to the following: Death by strangulation with a man's tie made of polyester and wool materials, tightly woven. Victim had been in good physical shape prior to strangulation. Time of death: 8:00 a.m. to 8:30 a.m., most likely closer to 8:00 a.m. The only DNA found on the tie was the victim's own.

The detective sighed and thought, there goes my belief that the tie had been the assailant's. But for it to have belonged to Dean made no sense. The man showed up at the beach in sweatpants, windbreaker, and flip-flops. Why would he have been wearing a tie? Also, according to the bed and breakfast lady, Dean left her establishment not wearing a tie that morning. She had been sure about that. Since the sole DNA on that tie was his own, he must have brought it along himself. But why?

He shook his head, thinking, this case may be more complicated than simple blackmail gone wrong. The suspects I've interviewed so far gave me some vague ideas, but nothing has come to light that I can sink my teeth into, the detective reflected. Granted, I've learned that Justin Picard was a bully. Would that be a motive for murder? It could be, if one of his bullying targets had been pushed to the limit.

Then he read the result of Dean Rickey's background check, which had also arrived that day. It stated that both parents of the victim had died, that Dean Rickey had been their only child, that he had been married and divorced, and that he had no children. In short, the man had no known living person next of kin. He mused, the poor guy has nobody who mourns him but that's not my problem.

Lastly, he was reading the police report from three decades ago about Justin Picard's death. The bottom line was that the boy's jump had been pronounced a suicide.

Scharfkopf sighed again and thought, I have a few more people on Sister Margaret's list of classmates to question. I need to get some useful information from them. I can't picture myself retiring with an unsolved homicide case on my record.

That thought process led him to travel plans his wife had pressured him to agree to for December, immediately after his retirement. She had given him the choices of visiting the Weihnachtsmarkt in Stuttgart, Germany; a Caribbean cruise; or ten days of skiing and fun in the snow at North Shore Lake Tahoe. According to her, reservations needed to be made right away. The detective would have preferred to stay at home, go to a game or two, have a barbecue in their backyard weather permitting, and generally spend his time relaxing.

In the years of experience at his job, Scharfkopf had learned that sometimes it helped to let his mind concentrate on something else. So he spent the rest of the day clearing his desk of paperwork that had accumulated from other cases.

He was getting ready to go home when his phone rang.

It was the lady from the bed and breakfast, and she said, "You told me I should call if I remembered something."

"Yes?"

"It's about the tie," she said. "Late last Saturday night, past midnight as I recall, I saw Dean Rickey do something strange. Mind you, I was not spying on him, but we have a common guest restroom, since most of our rooms don't have private bathrooms."

"I get it," said the detective and thought, come to the point, lady.

She continued, "I'm a light sleeper and heard someone in the hallway, and since it was so late and all the guests were accounted for, I got up to investigate. I didn't think it was a burglar, but I grabbed a baseball bat, just in case."

After a pause she went on, "The door to the bathroom stood open and I saw Mr. Rickey in front of the mirror, tying and retying a tie several times, as if he was aiming for a perfect knot. It was strange seeing the man, standing in his pajamas, doing this. I thought that he might have some kind of a tie fetish and tiptoed away, as I didn't want to embarrass him."

"I see."

"When you came by the other day, I'd forgotten all about it and only thought of it today. I normally would never tell anything private about my guests, but since you asked whether he'd worn a tie the morning he was killed, I thought you may want to know. Besides, nothing can hurt the poor man any longer now."

Scharfkopf said, "You did the right thing by telling me. Thank you for your help," and they ended the call.

He sat, staring into space, reflecting on what this whole tie business could mean. After a couple of wrong scenarios, he hit the nail on the head. The killer must have ordered

Dean to bring a tie to show that he could tie a perfect knot. That made sense from the perpetrator's point of view, since he or she did not want to bring a murder weapon. But how could Dean have been persuaded to go along with such an order? There must have been a plausible reason to do so, but the detective could not see it.

CHAPTER 23

Detective Scharfkopf knew that showing up unannounced at Dercan in Irvine, asking to see Ray Winter, may not be productive. First thing Thursday morning, he called the man and asked for an appointment. The CIO could fit him in at 1:00 in the afternoon, so Scharfkopf drove to Escondido to talk with Martin Taylor first.

After Scharfkopf rang the bell to the condominium, Vito opened the door a crack and the detective immediately heard loud, intense piano playing coming from within. He showed his badge and Vito ushered him into the entry hall.

The detective raised his voice and said, "Mr. Taylor, I'm investigating Dean Rickey's homicide and need to question you," hoping the other would turn down the music.

Vito answered, "You had better talk with Martin, then."

"Oh, you're not him?"

"I'm Vito, Martin's husband."

"Sorry! I should have realized that the piano playing is live. I do know that Martin Taylor is a pianist." And as he followed Vito into the living room, he stated, "I don't want to interrupt Martin's concentration. I can wait until he has finished."

"That may take a long time. Have a seat. May I offer you a beverage?"

Scharfkopf declined and Vito said, "Martin is a bit high-strung right now, which always happens on days before a major performance."

They had been conversing at shouting volume to be heard above the piano playing coming from the adjacent room. As they stopped talking, the detective started to enjoy the music he heard and closed his eyes.

Several minutes had passed when Vito said, "You can't wait forever. He's not going to like it, but I'll interrupt him."

When there finally was silence, Scharfkopf almost regretted that the piano playing had stopped.

Coming face to face with Martin, it was clear that the man had thrown himself into his music a hundred percent. His hair was disheveled and he was perspiring.

The detective said, "Sorry for interrupting, but maybe you can use a break." And he added, "I thoroughly enjoyed the concert. Thank you for the treat!"

The intensity did not leave Martin's face as he stamped his foot and declared, "I'm not ready for the concert by a long shot."

Vito explained, "We're flying to New York tomorrow. Martin is performing at the Weil Recital Hall on Saturday."

It was evident that the detective had never heard of the place, so he added, "The hall is part of Carnegie Hall."

"Wow!"

"And I'm not ready," repeated Martin, and plopped himself onto an easy chair.

Vito immediately went to stand behind him and massaged his neck and shoulders. That did the trick and Martin started to relax, saying "Vito tells me that you're investigating Dean's homicide. Sorry, I can't help. I had nothing to do with his murder."

"I'm not accusing you of it but would like your input. I've talked with several people who sat at his table during your class reunion and know of the comments Dean made, especially the accusation he left you all with at the end of the evening. Please tell me your version of the events, as best as you can remember. I would like to compare it with the information I have in my notes."

Martin did as instructed. His story tallied with what the detective had learned from other suspects.

At the end he commented, "I resented Dean. He ruined a lovely evening with his preposterous allegation. Not only that, he stirred up painful memories for me."

Vito stopped the massage and quietly left the room, giving the other two privacy for the interview.

"As it turned out, Dean's allegation wasn't preposterous at all," said Scharfkopf.

Martin bent his head in agreement.

"What about those painful memories? Did they concern Justin Picard?"

He bent his head again, and when he lifted it, words came out of his mouth in a torrent. He seemed to relive the anguish from 30 years ago as he said, "Justin made fun of me because I was different. He tormented and ridiculed me in front of his buddies every chance he got. I told myself that he was an ignorant jock and didn't know any better, but it didn't help getting rid of the hurt."

Suddenly realizing who he was talking to, and why, Martin stated, "I was not sad when I heard that he was dead, but I didn't push him off the turret."

"Let's switch back to the present. What were you doing last Sunday morning, September 8, from 8:00 a.m. until 8:30 a.m.?"

Martin thought about it for a second and then said, "I was taking a ride."

"Where to?"

"Just around the neighborhood."

Scharfkopf demanded, "You can do better than that. Where did you go?"

"I'm telling the truth. I drove around the neighborhood for a while and then back home."

"Without stopping anywhere?"

"That's right."

"Why?"

"Taking a ride relaxes me. I didn't sleep well and had lain awake for hours. So I got up, ate some cereal, and then went for a ride."

The detective looked out the window, surveying the neighborhood, while he pondered the suspect's answer. Then he asked, "Was the reason you had trouble sleeping because you mulled over Dean's accusation?"

"Yes, but I also realized that my concert in New York was only a week away. I never sleep well days before a major performance."

"Did your husband come along for the ride?"

"Vito was asleep when I left and was about to wake up when I got back."

"At what time was that?"

"I didn't look at the time."

Vito came back into the living room and stated, "It was exactly 8:30 when I woke up and heard Martin return."

"Thanks for being accurate," Scharfkopf said, and thought that he must have been listening from the other room.

And getting on his feet, he spoke the standard words about not leaving the country.

He almost told Martin to 'break a leg' but felt it would be inappropriate and said instead, "Good luck to you at Carnegie Hall."

While walking to his car the detective thought, funny how Martin clenched his long, elegant fingers into a fist and unclenched them, over and over again, while he was being interviewed. It could be that he was exercising them after piano playing, or that he was nervous about being questioned by the police. Or, could it be out of guilt?

CHAPTER 24

Detective Scharfkopf arrived at Ray Winter's place of business at exactly one o'clock. The IT department was on the 4th floor of the Dercan building, and his office was set apart from the cubicles occupied by his team. On entering, and looking straight ahead, the detective saw three large monitors, all next to each other, sitting on a huge desk. The keyboard, as well as a laptop, rested on the desk's sliding shelf. The state-of-the-art office chair was unoccupied. Beyond the massive desk was a floor-to-ceiling window with a view to the city of Irvine.

Scharfkopf thought that he was alone in the man's office, when a voice came from behind a wall, saying, "Come in."

What he had taken as a paneled wall decoration was in fact a shoji screen partition, and on close examination, it even sported a door. As he stepped through, he found Ray seated on a barstool at what resembled a breakfast counter, taking the last bite from a pastrami sandwich. He judged the man to be in his late 50's, possibly not far from his own age.

Scharfkopf said, "Sorry to interrupt your meal, Mr. Winter." And he added, "I hope I didn't keep you from going out to lunch."

After swallowing, Ray replied, "Not at all. I'm done.
I have my food delivered more often than not; going out
wastes too much time."

He pointed to the stool next to him and beckoned,
"Have a seat." Then he looked at his smartwatch and said,
"I can give you 15 minutes."

"I'd better get on with it, then," said the detective. "I've
interviewed most of your wife's former classmates who
sat at the crucial table at the reunion, so we don't need to
go into what was discussed and the bombshell that Dean
Rickey unloaded."

Before Scharfkopf could continue, Ray remarked, "I
didn't really want to go to Lori's reunion. Now I wish we
hadn't gone."

"I see your point," the detective said. He went on, "I
understand that you taught at Seabreeze High. Tell me
how that came about."

"Sure. 30 years ago, computer science programs were
still in their infancy stage at high schools. I participated in
a trial enrichment program offered at local high schools,
sponsored by UC San Diego. For one semester, I taught a
course on computer programming at Seabreeze High, held
after school hours. Since there was only a short supply of
computers in the classroom, the course was limited to no
more than a dozen students. They had to sign up for it on
a first come, first serve basis. The program did not catch
on and was discontinued the next semester."

"Dean Rickey was in your class, correct?"

"He said so at the reunion, but I didn't remember him."

"Besides your wife, did you know any of the former
students seated at your table prior to the reunion?" asked
the detective.

"Just Angie – I mean, Sister Margaret – who is my
wife's close friend."

Scharfkopf inquired, "Were you teaching at Seabreeze High when Justin Picard fell to his death from the turret?"

"Yes, I was teaching the course when that happened."

"Did you know the boy?"

"I went to the school's football game once and saw him play quarterback. But no, I did not know him personally."

The detective said, "I've been told that the turret was known as *Lovers' Nest*, but what other functions did it have?"

"I have no idea," Ray replied. "There must have been a reason for its existence, but I never thought about it. The place was claustrophobic. Simply climbing the dark stairs leading up to it was challenging."

"Did you ever go up to the turret?"

"No. I had no reason to go there."

"Was your wife, then Lori Aames, one of your students?"

"No, sir."

"But you knew her?"

Ray was a bit embarrassed when he replied, "I met her the day after Justin died. She was sitting on a bleacher, sobbing, and I learned that she was the quarterback's girlfriend."

"So you were her comforter," the detective remarked.

"I felt sorry for the girl."

"And that feeling soon turned to romance?"

"Nothing like that," protested Ray. It took self-control for him not to raise his voice as he continued, "I was 29 and she was just a kid. We did not have a relationship. I sort of became her mentor, that's all. In fact, we did not date until Lori was a sophomore at UC San Diego. Although she was not a student in my class, relationships between faculty members and students were frowned upon. We kept ours a secret and only got married after I quit teaching and started working for Dercan."

Scharfkopf said, "You sort of mentored her into choosing UC San Diego. Do I have that right?"

There was charm in Ray's grin as he replied, "You see right through me."

"I understand that your wife had many admirers back in high school. There is something special about her to date. Even I was aware of it when I interviewed her the other day."

"She's one of a kind," agreed Ray. "And now that our twins are settled in college, I have her all to myself again."

"Speaking of Mrs. Winter, when I asked about her whereabouts on Sunday morning, September 8, from 8:00 a.m. until 8:30 a.m., she stated that she was out for a walk with Duke. She had no witnesses and said that you went back to the hotel that morning at around the same time. Why was that?"

Ray replied, "At the reunion the night before, my wedding band came off when I washed my hands in the hotel restroom. I placed it on the mirror ledge, then forgot about it. I went back to the hotel first thing Sunday morning to retrieve it, and luckily it was still where I'd left it."

"Who came back first?"

He thought about it for a second, then said, "I believe Lori and Duke came home moments ahead of me; she was hanging up the leash as I came into the entry."

There was a buzz coming from Ray's watch and he stated, "I have a Zoom meeting with my staff in five minutes since some people on my team are working remotely."

The detective got the hint and said, "In that case we're done. Thank you for your time," and they both got up from their stools and stepped back into the CIO's working section of the office. As Scharfkopf headed for the door, he could hear rapid clicking of keyboard keys behind him, and realized that Ray Winter had already put their entire discussion out of his mind.

CHAPTER 25

On Friday, September 13, Alex Kazarian was the last person left of the class reunion attendees to be interviewed. Scharfkopf put off driving all the way to Glendale, not because he was superstitious but because traffic was impractical on any given Friday. Instead, he entered the small escort service office in San Diego.

The lady behind the counter asked, "What can we help you with?"

"I'm looking for a woman by the name of Gigi."

"For tonight?"

"I'd like to have a word with her now."

"Gigi only works evenings, but we have daytime escorts. Let me see who's available."

He stopped her as she consulted her smartphone, and, showing his credentials said, "I'm Detective Scharfkopf. I need to question Gigi."

The lady turned hostile and stated, "We are doing nothing illegal here! Our young women are escorts, not prostitutes."

Scharfkopf held up his hand and said, "You misunderstand. Gigi is not in trouble. I need to interview her as a witness in a case I'm investigating."

Somewhat reassured, the lady informed him that Gigi had a daytime job at a florist and was kind enough to mention the shop's name.

Elegant Bunch was in San Diego's Gas Lamp District. When entering the flower shop, the detective faced a tall young woman who held down the fort alone.

He asked, "Are you Gigi?"

"Yeah. Who wants to know?"

"I'm Detective Scharfkopf. You must have heard about Dean Rickey's murder. I'm in charge of investigating the homicide."

"Who is Dean Rickey?"

"He engaged your services last Saturday evening."

"Oh him. I'd forgotten his name. And no, I didn't know. He was a big bore, but I'm sorry he got himself murdered."

Scharfkopf stated, "Most likely, you were the last person to see him alive."

"Hold on! I had nothing to do with any murder."

The bell chimed at the entrance and he said, "Go ahead and help your customer; I can wait."

While she took care of business, Scharfkopf looked around the place. There were numerous bouquets of assorted flowers in vases behind a glass door, but he preferred the simple roses that were presented in an array of colors. There was also a tropical plant section, with gentle steam blowing out of ducts to keep them moist.

When the customer left, Gigi glared at Scharfkopf and said, "I didn't know the dude and had no reason to kill him."

"I'm not accusing you, but maybe you can help me figure out who did."

Calmer now, she said, "I doubt it."

"I'm ignorant about the escort enterprise. Do people ask for a specific escort by name or does the office assign the person?"

"Either way works," she replied. "In this Dean whatever case, I received a call from the agency that someone needed an escort to a high school reunion. I accepted the job and that was that."

"Do you get paid by the hour or for an entire evening?"

She replied, "We have an hourly rate and touching is extra."

"What do you mean by touching?"

Gigi got impatient and shot back, "It means exactly what the word means. If there is physical contact involved, like linking arms, holding hands, or dancing, for instance, that would be touching." And she glared at him and stated, "Our agency is strictly for escorting people to functions, nothing more. We provide a respectable service."

"I didn't mean to imply anything else," he assured her, and thought he had better get back to discussing what he came to question her about before she became unreceptive.

He said, "I know the topics that were discussed during the evening of the reunion and the accusation Dean made at the end. You don't need to go into all that. I would like your input on what you thought of him."

Gigi stated, "He was a bore and tried to show off by making silly remarks about people. Some of it was awkward and trivial, but what he mentioned about one of the women was downright mean. I was sure that he hired me to impress the others, but I secretly laughed to myself because nobody was impressed."

"You don't take yourself too seriously," he said with a grin.

"I guess I don't, but I was mad when he got annoyed because I didn't know what a CIO is or had never heard of some famous high-tech company. So I didn't go to college and may not know a lot of stuff, but I'm holding down two jobs to make ends meet and have no time to keep up with things."

The phone rang, and soon she was busy taking down an order for delivery. After she ended the call he asked, "Are you the sole employee here?"

"The shop belongs to an elderly lady who comes twice a week to help me, and we have a delivery guy, but I'm pretty much on my own the rest of the time."

Getting back to the interview, the detective asked, "Did you come and go to the reunion in a taxi, or did you take an Uber?"

"No. Dean picked me up in his car and drove me back. The car had an Arizona license number, if you're interested."

"You may not keep up with current events, but you're observant," he complimented, and asked, "Do you remember what you talked about during the rides?"

"On the way to the hotel he seemed a bit nervous and didn't talk much. He mentioned that he may be able to relocate to California. And on the way back, he looked excited. To tell you the truth, I was tired and didn't pay attention. I just wanted to get home."

There was another call, and it came from Gigi's cellphone. Scharfkopf heard the lopsided conversation of, "Hi Mom. What's up? - - Oh? - - Give him Tylenol. I'll try to leave early. - - Sure. Thanks, Mom."

"Anything wrong?" asked the detective.

"My four-year-old son is sick and has a temperature. My mother had to pick him up from day care."

She noticed the surprise on his face and said, "Yeah, I was a teenage mom and kept the baby. Now I'm paying the price, but I wouldn't trade him for a college education or anything else in the world."

"Just one last question," he said. "Did Dean leave the table to go outdoors to smoke?"

"More than once. Come to think of it, the last time he did, he was gloating when he got back."

"Did anyone else leave the table at the same time?"

She thought about it and then said, "Sorry, I don't remember."

He did not ask her where she was on Sunday morning between 8:00 and 8:30, since he did not consider her a suspect, but bought nine long-stemmed red roses to bring home to his wife.

CHAPTER 26

While the Kazarians ate breakfast on Monday morning, September 16, Alex said, "I meant to tell you but forgot. The detective in charge of Dean Rickey's murder investigation called Friday. He's coming to our Glendale location today to interview me."

Michelle, toast in hand, looked up from reading the paper and asked, "Whose murder and what detective?"

"Pay attention. Dean was at the reunion and was killed the very next day. We heard about the murder on the local evening news that Sunday, when we watched TV at the hotel in Seabreeze, remember?"

"Sure, I remember. But why do the authorities want to interview you? Didn't you tell them that you had nothing to do with it?"

"If you recall, Dean accused one of us former classmates of pushing Justin from the turret in our high school days, and not even 12 hours later, he himself gets murdered. The detective - - and by the way, it's only one man, not 'the authorities' - - must consider every one of us a suspect."

Michelle finished her toast and drank her coffee, folded the paper neatly, and then commented, "Well, I wasn't around at your high school 30 years ago and met Dean Rickey for the first time at your class reunion, so I'm sure this police officer doesn't need to talk with me."

"Probably not, but in case he does, he's coming to the Glendale car wash, where you can make yourself available."

As usual, Michelle had the last word and remarked, "Obviously, I cannot possibly be considered a suspect in either murder, and since you are innocent as well, you have nothing to worry about. So stop being so nervous."

CHAPTER 27

During his drive to Glendale on that Monday morning, Detective Scharfkopf had plenty of time to mull things over. The weekend had been productive as far as his private life was concerned. He had agreed to take a Caribbean cruise, as long as his wife took care of all the arrangements, including purchasing new luggage. Of the three choices she had proposed, he felt a cruise came closest to relaxing in his own back yard.

"Productive," however, was not the word he'd use when thinking of Dean Rickey's homicide investigation. Yesterday was exactly one week since he had been called to the scene at The Cove, and he was not anywhere near solving the case. Sure, he knew how the murder was done and that the motive was to silence a blackmailer for witnessing a crime that took place 30 years ago. Trying to reconstruct a cold case three decades later was something he'd never had to deal with before.

After having gotten away with the crime for so many years, it must have been a shock to the killer to suddenly come face to face with a witness. The person must be quick-witted to have been able to plan the silencing of the accuser on the spur of the moment and execute it the very next day.

He tried to put himself into the mind of the murderer and mulled over what must have happened at that reunion after the guilty person became aware that Dean Rickey had witnessed the crime. The culprit most likely followed Dean outdoors when he went for a cigarette break, and the two planned to meet at The Cove the next morning. The idea to use a tie as the murder weapon must have entered the killer's mind right then and there. It had to be Dean's own tie because of the DNA angle. But how was it possible to have Dean comply without arousing his suspicion? There had to be a plausible explanation but Scharfkopf failed to see it.

At that point of his musing, he arrived in Glendale and followed the GPS instructions to the car wash facility.

On arrival, Alex Kazarian first proudly took him on a tour of his business. To the detective's surprise, there were no machines to be seen at the place. Everything was done by hand in a most efficient way.

Alex accompanied him from station to station, where a car first got rinsed off with a hose, then driven to the next space where the actual washing took place. This was done with two buckets: one filled with soap suds for shampooing, the other with clear water for rinsing. The workers used two separate microfiber mitts for the washing and rinsing. One employee climbed a step ladder to reach the roof of a car with his mitt.

Next in line was the worker who dried the vehicle with a microfiber cloth. Detailing followed by removing soap residue and cleaning swirls with a clay bar, and special attention was given to tires by scrubbing them with a brush. Lastly, employees took care of the inside by vacuuming and wiping the dashboard, console, and doors. All glass was cleaned, including windshield, windows, and rearview mirrors.

This concluded the 'show and tell,' and while the two walked to Alex's office, Scharfkopf remarked, "I'm impressed. You clearly own the *crème de la crème* of car washes."

"Thanks," said Alex, beaming with pride. And he joked, "I would have offered to treat your car to a wash, but that might look like bribery."

The office was modest but comfortable, with a couple of upholstered chairs and Alex's desk, which was located by a window so that he had a clear view to car wash activities while seated behind it. There was a small refrigerator in the room and Alex offered the detective a beverage, which he declined. Then they got down to business.

He asked, "What can you tell me about Justin Picard?"

"He was a bully but also a coward."

"How so?"

"He harassed kids, but nobody could get even with him since he always kept a bunch of buddies around. You could never get him alone."

"Did you have cause to get even?"

"Sure, but I wasn't the only one. If you must know, he put me down for being Armenian."

Scharfkopf said, "How did that come about?"

"It was a stupid remark he made, but it pissed me off. I made the mistake of talking to his girlfriend and - - -"

"Would that have been Lori?"

"So you've been told that she was his girlfriend. Anyhow, I talked to the girl, nothing more. She was nice to everybody, by the way. Justin didn't approve, the jerk. He came up to me and said, 'Stay away from Lori. She isn't interested in any Armenian.'"

"That must have made you angry," said Scharfkopf.

"It did, and I'd have liked to punch him but as I said, he was never alone."

"Now let's talk about Dean Rickey. Did you believe his claim that he saw someone push Justin from the turret?"

"I wasn't sure whether he'd made it up. It seemed far-fetched to come forward after so many years. On the other hand, I was initially surprised that Justin committed suicide. I didn't think he was the type. And now it looks like someone did find him alone up at the turret." He raised both hands and added, "It wasn't me."

The window was open a few inches and the detective could hear the sloshing of cars being washed, while Alex seemed far away with his thoughts and suddenly said, "It doesn't make sense, though."

"What doesn't?"

"Why would he be up at the turret all by himself?"

The detective knew that no answer was expected and posed his routine question, asking, "Where were you Sunday morning, September 8, from 8:00 a.m. until 8:30 a.m.?"

Alex was ready with his answer and stated, "My wife and I stayed at the hotel in Seabreeze for two nights after the reunion. On Sunday morning, I drove to San Diego and went to Kobey's Swap Meet at the Sports Arena. I was there during the time you mentioned." And he asked, "Was that when Dean was killed?"

Scharfkopf ignored the question and continued, "Is going to swap meets something you do regularly?"

"Yes, sir. I'm a collector of bronzes and my wife has a collection of Hummel figurines."

"So your wife went with you to Kobey's?"

"No. She slept in."

The detective scratched his head and inquired, "So what did you buy?"

"Actually, nothing. I looked at some Hummels, but didn't make a purchase."

"At what time did you leave the hotel and when did you return?"

"I left a few minutes before eight and got back before ten, in time to have breakfast with Michelle."

"Do you have a witness that can place you at the swap meet during the crucial time?"

"I can do better than that," said Alex, and grabbed his phone. He scrolled down his texts, then showed the detective a picture of a figurine while stating, "I found this rare Hummel at the swap meet and texted about it to my wife. She texted back, mentioning that she already had the piece in her collection, so of course I didn't buy it."

He beamed at the detective and said, "Look at the date and time of the text!"

Scharfkopf confirmed that the text was sent on September 8 at 8:24, and he said, "Looks like you have an alibi, Mr. Kazarian."

On the way out of the place, he waved to Michelle Kazarian, who sat at the cashier window, doing a crossword puzzle in between taking care of customers.

Once in his car, Scharfkopf thought back to Alex's probing into why Justin would have been up on the turret alone and told himself, that's a good question. And something else occurred to him. The man he just interviewed had been more than ready with his alibi. The way he proved that he was at Kobey's swap meet at the appropriate time by showing the text message almost seemed rehearsed.

Then he pondered that he now had talked with all suspects and the next thing to do would involve looking at his notes. Since that needed to wait until he got to his desk, it was best to put the investigation out of his mind.

He tuned into a radio station he was comfortable with and listened to classic rock all the way back to San Diego.

CHAPTER 28

Looking over his notes, Scharfkopf realized that Sister Margaret was the only suspect who had a verified alibi. He had spoken with the other two nuns she had mentioned. Both confirmed that the three had attended Sunday Mass together, which started at eight o'clock and lasted an hour.

As for the others, Dong Kim could have walked or even driven over to The Cove after checking out the snorkeling equipment rental place. Heather Jones-Levine had no alibi at all, since she claimed to have been asleep. Lori Aames-Winter had no witness to her walking the dog, nor for the time she left and came back, as her husband drove to the hotel at approximately the same time. Raphael Torres only had his wife to confirm that he was home, eating breakfast, at the crucial time. Martin Taylor had no one to support his claim that he drove around the neighborhood.

The next person on his notes of people he had interviewed was Ray Winter. Even though he had not known Justin Picard, nor remembered Dean Rickey having been his student, he had been present at Seabreeze High during the crucial semester that the former fell, or rather was pushed, from the turret. Ray Winter's alibi was that he went to retrieve his wedding band from the hotel. Scharfkopf had checked up on that. The concierge confirmed having spoken to Ray when he was on the way to the hotel restroom. Theoretically, he could have made a detour to The Cove after leaving the hotel.

Gigi was not a suspect since the detective was sure that Dean's murder was a consequence of the crime committed three decades ago, before the young woman was even born. He learned some interesting facts from her, though.

Alex Kazarian's text, proving that he was at Kobey's swap meet on September 8 at 8:24, seemed to be a perfect alibi on first sight. On deeper reflection, Scharfkopf concluded that with Sunday morning's traffic being light, it might have taken only ten minutes to drive from Seabreeze to San Diego. Alex could have gone to The Cove first, strangled Dean Rickey, and then driven to Kobey's.

Tackling motive was tricky. It stood to reason that the motive for killing Dean was blackmail. It also stood to reason that figuring out the motive for the dormant crime was essential. In Lori and Heather's case, the motive would have revolved around a love triangle. As for the four men - - boys at the time of the murder - - it would have had to be getting even with the bully. Scharfkopf could not come up with a motive for the professor.

As far as opportunity for that first murder, any of the suspects could have either had a rendezvous with Justin at the turret, or followed him up. The killing of Justin happened after school hours, and both girls had admitted to having been up there with him on the day of the tragedy. Both also claimed that they had left him alive. Either one could be lying. There was also no way of knowing in what order those two rendezvous took place.

If the murderer was not one of the girls, a third person must have gone up to meet him later. That meeting may have been planned. Why else would Justin stay at the turret by himself? According to Alex Kazarian's statement, the boy could never be found without his buddies.

Scharfkopf then mulled things over from a different angle. In Dean's case, the culprit could easily have been a woman. Strangling someone with a tie did not require much strength, especially if the victim was taken by surprise. As for pushing someone off the turret, a football player no less, that may have taken a greater effort. He would have to look at the place for himself, he decided.

CHAPTER 29

Detective Scharfkopf had an appointment to see the principal of Seabreeze High on the next day. The woman was in her forties and could not have been at her post during Justin Picard's days at the school. Still, when he referred to the investigation during their phone conversation, she had graciously offered to show him the campus.

He got there mid-morning while classes were in progress. Her office was in the administration building close to the entrance of the school.

From there, while guiding him along the outside of the one-story buildings that housed the classrooms, she asked, "I'm aware that you are interested in a suicide that happened at the school way before my time here, but what exactly are you looking for?"

"I want to familiarize myself with the building that houses your turret, and the structures around it," replied the detective.

"Good, so we don't have to disturb anyone in the classrooms," she said, and marched him - - high heels clapping with every step - - to the centralized two-story structure.

One side of the building's ground floor accommodated the auditorium, the other housed the cafeteria. The teacher's lounge and music rooms sat on the second floor.

A walkway and wide stairs connected the two. The turret was part of that connection and towered over the roof of the building by 10 feet. It gave the structure a dramatic effect from an architect's perspective, but what its function was meant to be was anyone's guess.

As they stood at the base of the turret Scharfkopf said, "I need to go up to conduct my investigation."

"We keep the door to it locked. I'll text the custodian. Let's go to the teacher's lounge while we wait for him," and they climbed the stairs to the second floor. Once there, she offered a cup of coffee, which he accepted, and they sat down near a window. There was no one else in the room since all the teachers were in class at the moment.

Scharfkopf stated, "I'm surprised that the door to the turret is locked. It is my understanding that students had free access to it 30 years ago."

"Maybe so, but ever since I've worked here, we've kept it under lock and key."

He sipped his coffee and looked out the window. Having a clear view down to the entrance of the turret, he thought that the door to it looked somewhat out of place. There was nothing wrong with its fit, but he had the strange feeling that it didn't belong.

The principal said, "I've heard about the suicide, but that was so long ago. Why is there an investigation now?"

"Something has come to light recently which makes the boy's fall a possible homicide," stated the detective. Unwilling to go any further with the topic, he was glad the janitor showed up at that moment. He gulped down the coffee and got to his feet.

After introducing the man, the principal said, "I'll leave you two to explore the turret. If you need anything else, Detective Scharfkopf, I'll be in my office," and she made her exit.

While the two men walked back down the stairs Scharfkopf asked, "How long have you been the janitor at Seabreeze High?"

"Seven years, but I prefer to be called 'custodian.'"

After the custodian unlocked the door, the detective asked, "Has this door to the turret always existed?"

"Ever since I've worked here," was the reply. And he said, "I'm kinda busy, do you need me at the turret?"

"Not at all. I'll find my way up."

"Make sure you lock the door from the inside when you get back," the man said, and was gone.

As he climbed the steep, circular steps in the gloomy stairway, Scharfkopf wished he had brought a flashlight. No wonder someone had mentioned that the place was claustrophobic. When he reached the top, he found the small spot, outfitted with a miniscule table and a bench with no cushioning, solely the hard, raw wood. There was no window, only three walls with an opening to the small balcony. How anyone could have named the uncomfortable place *Lovers' Nest* was a puzzle to him.

He stepped onto the balcony and was treated to a great view of Seabreeze and the ocean beyond. He doubted that the kids would have had a great interest in the view, though. He measured the approximate height of the railing around the balcony with his hands and judged it to be about three feet high.

Granted, the railing wasn't high, but could a girl hoist someone over it? he wondered. With a bit of a run-up it would be possible but there was no room for a run-up in the small space. The element of surprise might have also worked. Still, Justin was a quarterback, which meant that he'd have been agile and strong enough to catch the balustrade and hold on to it, preventing the fall. What if he was a show-off and pulled himself up to the railing for fun and dare? Pushing him off in that case would have been easy as pie.

He shook his head and thought, I was hoping to eliminate the girls from my list of suspects, but now I can't.

CHAPTER 30

The principal had been kind enough to give Scharfkopf the name and number of the retired custodian. The man lived at the outskirts of San Diego, and the detective found him mowing the lawn in his front yard in the late afternoon of Wednesday, September 18.

The robust 72-year-old didn't mind interrupting his chore and said, "My wife is watching the grandkids in the house. I think we have more peace and quiet outside," and walked him to the backyard to a set of garden furniture.

After they settled into a couple of lawn chairs, the scent of fresh cut grass entered Scharfkopf's nostrils as he asked, "How is retirement treating you?"

"Can't complain," the other replied, "but every so often I still miss Seabreeze High."

"I visited the school yesterday. It's a fine campus, but I was wondering about the door leading up to the turret. Was it always there?"

The former custodian chuckled and said, "So you've noticed that it looks out of place. Way back, in the first few years of my employment at the school, there was no door. You stepped through an open entry before heading up the stairs. After the kid jumped from up there, they added the door and I kept it locked."

"Speaking of that boy, I understand that you found him. Tell me how that came about."

"It was a horrible sight. Even after all these years, the hairs on my neck stand up, thinking about it." He found his composure and continued, "I remember it was on a Tuesday and - - -"

"You can still recall that it was Tuesday?"

"Tuesdays were always late working days for me since lots of after-school activities took place."

"Sorry for interrupting," said Scharfkopf, "please go on."

"I had to wait to lock up until everything was done."

"What kind of activities were held after school hours?"

The retired custodian counted on his fingers, "There was football practice out on the field. They played basketball in the gym. The drama kids were rehearsing their fall play in the auditorium. The professor's computer class was held in one of the classrooms; in another, the science club students got together - - I called them the smarty pants. And there was choir practice in a music room. That's all I remember off hand."

He paused, then stated, "Like I said, it was late - - probably around seven o'clock or even later - - as it was already dark by the time I finally made the rounds to lock up. I decided to take a shortcut across the lawn when walking over to my parking space in the lot. The nightlights surrounding the campus had already come on, and from a distance I thought that an animal was laying in the grass. As I got closer, I realized that it was a boy and started to run toward him, but he was beyond help."

The seasoned man swallowed hard before he continued, "His body was all twisted and I could tell that he had a broken neck. There was a lot of blood too. I almost puked while running back to the administration building to call

911." He added, "It goes without saying that we didn't have cellphones at the time."

Scharfkopf asked, "Was the boy laying on his back or stomach when you found him?"

"Neither, he was on his side and all twisted, like I already said." He thought, what difference does it make how he landed? Aloud he asked, "Why are you looking into this so many years later?"

Scharfkopf was unwilling to discuss the current homicide investigation of Dean Rickey and replied, "New evidence came to light suggesting that the boy's death was murder, not suicide."

That settled, the detective said, "Thank you. Your input gives me lots of food for thought," and got up to leave, while the septuagenarian headed to the front yard to finish mowing his lawn.

On his drive away, Scharfkopf thought, so I can forget my theory about the position Justin Picard landed on – or can't I?

CHAPTER 31

Detective Scharfkopf sat in his office with the door closed - - oblivious to the hustle and bustle going on in the rest of his department - - mulling over what he had learned from his visit to the high school and his talk with the retired custodian.

Going with the concept that Justin Picard had been pushed from the turret, rather than jumped, the detective tried to reconstruct the fall.

If pushed from the back, he would have landed on his stomach, face down. And assuming he had been facing the assailant when pushed, he most likely would have hit the pavement on his back. The first scenario might have been a surprise attack, possibly from one of the female suspects. The other could have been during a fistfight with a guy. But according to the retired custodian, Justin lay on his side when he found him, meaning that the boy altered his position during the fall.

This is getting me nowhere, concluded Scharfkopf. I need to look at it from a different angle. Both girls, Lori and Heather, thought that they had been the last person to see Justin alive. Each woman made it clear during their interviews that Justin was alive and stayed at the turret by himself when they left. If one of them was lying, it would help if he could figure out in which order they were up at Lovers' Nest. Both said it had been after school hours; Heather was not specific and Lori stated that it had been after choir practice. 30 years later, it was impossible to determine the exact time of their respective rendezvous.

And if they were telling the truth, the killer went up to the turret later, finding Justin alone. But why would he stay there by himself? Had he arranged to settle a score up there? That seemed out of character. According to more than one person, the bully always had his buddies with him. It didn't make sense that the killer would look for him up at the turret.

Something had occurred to Scharfkopf when sitting at the teacher's lounge, looking down to the base of the turret. Now what was it? he now tried to remember.

Frustrated, he thought, I'm grasping at straws. I should be farther along with the investigation by now. I had better come up with a brainstorm or evidence. I'm going to end up retiring with an unsolved homicide on my record unless I start doing my job.

CHAPTER 32

Scharfkopf's wife dragged him to the travel agent the next day. He had told her that he was too busy, and whether she had forgotten that she was in charge of their cruise. She stood her ground, reminding him that the travel agent had recommended that it would be beneficial to have them both come for an orientation appointment before the actual booking of the trip, especially since they had never been on a cruise before. In the end, he decided that getting his mind off the Dean Rickey case for a while may not be a bad idea after all.

Once at the travel agency, they first learned about the different ports where the ship would stop and the excursions people could sign up for at each. Next, the agent went into detail about the activities and entertainment offered on board.

"There's something for everyone," she said, "whether swimming and water games, ping-pong, darts, shuffleboard, or lawn bowling - - all is available, and more. There are art classes, and of course you can play all sorts of table games. At night there is music and dancing, and you can attend a spectacular show. Or, if you prefer just to relax, you can bask in the sun on a lounge chair on deck."

Scharfkopf thought, now you're talking!

She continued, "It goes without saying that there is Las Vegas style gambling in the ship's casino. And I'm sure you must have heard from friends who cruise that the food on board is excellent. If you have any special dietary needs, let the crew know ahead of time so that the chef can be informed."

She looked at Scharfkopf and asked, "Any questions?"

"Just one," he said. "What's it going to cost?"

"I was getting to that. The price depends on which cabin you choose. Your wife already mentioned her preference for a balcony stateroom and I temporarily reserved one for you. But to be fair to you, sir, I held off on the final booking, waiting for your approval."

She showed them pictures for each and said, "Here is a standard interior room with no window to the outside. The promenade view room has bay windows. In the ocean view cabins there is more living space, and there is an outside window. The most popular, and the one your wife favors, is the balcony stateroom, offering a private balcony."

There was an amount listed at the bottom of each photo. Naturally, his wife had picked the most expensive one.

He said, "Go ahead and make the final booking on the balcony stateroom."

"Excellent choice," said the agent. "Some people find the standard interior cabins claustrophobic."

She went on telling them about what to expect when leaving and re-entering ship at ports, concerning passports, et cetera, and what to do or not do on group excursions. She also mentioned luggage and tipping the crew at the end, but Scharfkopf no longer paid attention.

The word "claustrophobic" that she mentioned had triggered something which had dwelled in his subconscious. Now it sparked an entire new train of thought. He watched his wife writing a check, then stashing a folder with cruise information into her large bag before they got up to leave, but he was oblivious to all that, as his mind was elsewhere.

CHAPTER 33

On Friday, September 20, Angie, aka Sister Margaret, sent a group email to the former classmates who had been seated at her table at the reunion. It read:

"Hi all,

"Has anyone heard what the status is on Dean's homicide investigation? I assume that there hasn't been an arrest or it would have been in the news. The reason I am concerned is that we were told by the detective not to leave the country, and I am scheduled to start my foreign mission at the end of the month. That is in 10 days!

"During Detective Scharfkopf's questioning, I suggested that the crime may have been committed by an outsider, maybe someone from Arizona who followed Dean to Seabreeze. The more I think about it, the more that makes sense. I have a hard time believing that it was one of us.

"If any of you heard something, please let me know.

"Best regards,

"Angie"

There were responses within the next two days. All were in the negative as far as having heard anything.

Her friend Lori wrote, "Ray says that Scharfkopf is dragging his feet, but I think these investigations take time. I'm keeping my fingers crossed that your idea about it being an outsider is right. As for leaving the country,

I'm sure the detective can make an exception in your case. After all, you're a nun.

"PS: Will I see you before you leave?"

Raphael's lines read, "I have no news about the investigation. I hope that you are right about an outsider being the killer, but I doubt it. I wish you the best with your mission, dear Angie."

Dong's email was short and to the point, "Haven't heard. It stands to reason that the killer must be one of us."

Heather wrote, "If Detective Scharfkopf is making progress, he's certainly not letting us know about it. And you are right, if there was an arrest, it would have been in the news. As for someone from Arizona having murdered Dean, that is wishful thinking. Go do your thing and don't worry about the man's order not to leave the country. What's he going to do? Confiscate your passport?"

Alex's input was, "I am not expecting to hear or know the detective's progress. He is not obligated to share it with us. After all, we are suspects. But the man is smart and I bet he is close to making an arrest. Logic dictates that someone sitting at our table at the reunion is the culprit. As for leaving the country, I don't think he is allowed to keep you here, unless he has evidence that you are involved in the crime. So, bon voyage!"

Martin wrote, "I am trying hard to forget what happened to Dean. To tell you the truth, I almost managed to put it behind me, since I have been busy with concerts. About leaving the country, my European tour starts at the beginning of October, and I won't ask for permission to go."

CHAPTER 34

Detective Scharfkopf woke up in the middle of the night, remembering what the word "claustrophobic" had triggered in his mind when spoken by the travel agent. He realized now that it had to do with the dark, confining staircase leading up to the turret. Instead of falling back to sleep, he also dwelled on the day he had visited Seabreeze High. He now recalled the thought that had briefly entered his consciousness as he sat in the teacher's lounge, having a clear view down to the base of the turret.

Then he remembered fragments of conversations during interviews with suspects. The words "all to myself" seemed natural enough at the time they were spoken, but now he saw them in a different light.

Sleepless time went by as he reconstructed Justin Picard's murder, the way he felt certain it must have happened. In a weird way, the motive he had in mind also made sense. There was no chance of proving it, though. He had no evidence and, after so many years, there was none. He couldn't even come up with circumstantial evidence. What he had was nothing more than a hunch, yet he felt that he was finally on the right track.

Dean Rickey, the blackmailer, might have had something other than money in mind with his demand. What needed to be done now was to trap his killer. In other words, find a mole. Sister Margaret was the only one of the bunch with a tight alibi, but there was no way he could ask a nun to be the plant. He chuckled when picturing Mother Superior saying, "You want to use one of my sisters to do *what?*"

His wife stirred next to him and murmured, "What's funny?"

"Nothing. Go back to sleep."

Scharfkopf for his part was wide awake. It was already dawn when he came up with a plan and kept his fingers crossed that it would work.

CHAPTER 35

On Saturday morning Scharfkopf entered the Elegant Bunch florist shop once more. Gigi was helping customers so he waited patiently until the last one left.

She took the initiative and said, "You're not here to buy more flowers for your wife, correct?"

He nodded.

"I told you everything I know and have nothing more to add."

He stated, "I am asking for your help in my investigation and have a proposition. We can't pay you for your service but you might get satisfaction in knowing that you are contributing to bringing a criminal to justice."

She was amused and said, "Go on."

"I am 99% sure that I know who Dean Rickey's killer is but can't prove it. I would like to trap the person into admitting guilt, and with your help it may happen."

"So you want me to become a spy?"

"Something like that, yes."

"Tell me what's involved," she said.

"You need to contact the culprit and arrange a meeting. At that meeting I would like you to tell the perpetrator that Dean was a bit drunk on the drive home and told you the name of the person who killed Justin."

"Oh yeah, Justin was the kid he talked about having not jumped from some tower but was pushed. I thought he made that up, but now I realize it must be true."

Then she thought about it and asked, "By contacting the person, do you mean with a phone call or email? I don't like to give out my number or email address."

"You'll do none of that. I've formed our plan in detail. You will write a handwritten note and give it to me. My team will do the rest."

"I see."

Scharfkopf continued, "Getting back to the meeting. You will hint that you figured out Dean's blackmailing act. I will give you more details but first need to know whether you agree to help out."

Gigi became serious now and asked, "So you want me to pretend to do a little blackmailing of my own?"

"Correct."

"He's going to try to silence me too."

"We will not let it come to that. My team of law enforcers, myself included, will have your back."

A customer walked in and the detective made himself scarce, browsing the flower shop, while Gigi took care of business.

As soon as the shopper had left, she asked, "When is this going to happen?"

"We would like to get things rolling right away. How late do you work tomorrow?"

"I don't work at all. Sundays and Mondays are my days off here, and I also take myself off the availability list at the escort service for the two days, so my son and I can have some quality time together."

"Excellent timing."

"Yeah. I'd rather not tell my employers about it."

There was a pause while she thought about the proposal. Then she looked him in the eye and stated, "Okay, I'm in."

He asked, "About your son, can you arrange for him to stay with someone else for a few days? What's his name, by the way?"

"His name is Kenny. He can stay with my mom tomorrow and I can put him in daycare on Monday, but what do you mean by 'for a few days'? I thought you only needed me tomorrow and Monday."

"Your service will be for the two days, but to be on the cautious side, Kenny should stay with your mother and not go to daycare until we make an arrest. We hope this will be within the two days, but should it take longer, we want to make sure he is safe. This is simply a precaution; the perpetrator does not even know your last name, nor that you have a son."

Scharfkopf saw worry in Gigi's eyes as soon as he'd mentioned Kenny's safety. She seemed reassured, however, when she realized that the guilty person knew nothing about her.

So he kept on, "As to the location for your rendezvous, we can talk about it. It should be a public place with lots of people around, like the Zoo or SeaWorld, for instance."

"Or a mall," she put in.

"Good idea! Choose a mall that you are familiar with."

"I'd like the Mission Valley Mall," she said, and then asked, "Am I going to be wired?"

"Affirmative. That was one of the things I was going to bring up but you beat me to it," he said with a chuckle. Then he immediately got serious again as he stated, "Like I said, we are going to have your back all the way."

Gigi was getting excited and admitted, "I've always wondered what it would be like to work under cover."

He prompted, "Okay, I'll go ahead and brief you now."

But it took a few more interruptions before the briefing took place. The young delivery man needed instructions about where to go, she answered a phone call, and another customer walked in.

CHAPTER 36

On that evening Gigi asked Kenny, "How would you like a sleepover at grandma and grandpa's?"

"Yippee!" he yelled.

Once they got to her parent's house, things didn't go all that smoothly. Her father was out running errands, but her mother was full of curiosity, bombarding her with questions.

Kenny ran immediately to the room and closet where his toys were kept, while she got as far as the hallway, where her mother said, "Naturally, we'll keep Kenny here for as long as you want, but you were vague over the phone. Are you seeing someone? I was praying for the day that you'd finally start dating. What's he like? Has he met Kenny yet? Our grandson needs a father figure to look up to."

"Stop, Mom! And no, I'm not 'seeing someone.' I can't tell you what I'm doing, only that it's best if Kenny stays with you and Dad for a couple days, maybe a bit longer."

They had made it to the living room as her mother threw both arms up in the air and exclaimed, "Oh no! You're into something illegal."

"Just the opposite, I'm helping out law enforcement."

"You mean the police?"

"Yes," said Gigi, "they asked me to go under cover to help them with a case, but sorry, I can't tell you about it."

"Sounds fishy to me. They're probably impersonating police officers and are crooks."

"No, Mom. They're the real thing. And please don't ask me anything more."

"Well, if they're for real, that means what you're undertaking is dangerous." She raised her arms again and cried out, "Kenny may end up an orphan!"

Her grandson entered the living room as she uttered that last word, and he asked, "What's an orphan?"

Gigi didn't lose a beat and said, "Grandma meant 'oven.' She needs to check the oven," and gave her mom a nasty look.

Her son was no longer interested and asked, "Can I watch TV?"

"A little later. Go and build with your Legos."

"Okay," said Kenny and left them.

Once the women were by themselves again, Gigi said, "Don't be melodramatic. I know what I'm doing and so do the police in charge. I'll be totally safe, so don't worry. I appreciate that you'll take care of Kenny." She pointed to the duffle bag she had carried in and added, "It will most likely only be for two days, but I brought extra clothing for him, just in case."

Then she gave her mom a hug and said, "I've got to run. Say hi to Dad for me."

In the adjacent room she kissed her little boy good-bye and left.

CHAPTER 37

Among Saturday's mail, which had been dropped into the mailbox by the postal carrier, the perpetrator found an envelope addressed with first and last name only, and no street address or postal stamp. The letter had obviously been hand-carried. Luckily, the person whose name was on it was the one going to the mailbox that day, so no explanation needed to be made to a spouse. The note inside the envelope was hand-written and read:

"The wine Dean Rickey drank at the class reunion made him confide in me on our drive home that night. He told me that you were Justin Picard's killer. I could go to the police with my knowledge, but that wouldn't be profitable.

"Meet me tomorrow, Sunday afternoon, at two o'clock at the Mission Valley Mall in San Diego. I'll be waiting for you at the sitting area close to the Movie Theater.

"Gigi"

Who the heck is Gigi? the person thought at first glance at the note. Then remembrance kicked in: Oh yes, it's the young woman who looked like a model that Dean brought along. So the idiot blabbed to her and dropped my name. It stands to reason that this Gigi person is also trying to blackmail me. Dean is dead, so it's her word against mine, making it circumstantial evidence at best.

At first, the person was going to ignore the accusation note which had been dropped in their mailbox, but moments later had a change of mind. The prudent thing to do was to meet with her and find out what she really knew. Should it turn out that the woman lacked incriminating evidence, she would be ridiculed and the chapter was closed. And if she was accurate, she needed to be stopped.

The person then spent a good part of Saturday evening deciding what excuse to come up with to the spouse for canceling their Sunday afternoon plans.

CHAPTER 38

The underground parking garage at the Mission Valley Mall was filling up rapidly on a Sunday afternoon, but Gigi found a spot near the elevators. Her favorite stores were Nordstrom Rack, Francesca's, and Gamestop. However, on Sunday, September 22, coming off the elevator onto the open-air shopping mall, she headed straight for the AMC Theatres.

She was wired and Detective Scharfkopf's team was in place, although not visible.

There was ample space for privacy at the sitting area close to the theater, since most people came to the mall to shop or see a movie and not to socialize. Gigi was a couple of minutes early and watched folks walk by, the majority seeming to be in a hurry. Her adversary showed up at exactly two o'clock.

The person sat down next to her and to the passers-by it looked like the two had a friendly get-together. Their rendezvous was anything but friendly, though.

The perpetrator hissed, "Tell me what you know."

"As I said in my note, Dean Rickey told me that you killed that boy at Seabreeze High 30 years ago. He said he was a witness. His tongue was a bit loosened by the wine he drank at the reunion, and he babbled on about needing to make a proper tie knot."

"What else?"

"He said that you suggested meeting at The Cove to take care of business. Obviously, that was the meeting place where you strangled him with his own tie."

There was menace in the person's voice, as they uttered, "That was two weeks ago. Why did you wait until now to contact me?"

Gigi said, "I usually don't keep up with current events but a few days ago I sat in the dentist's waiting room and browsed through an old newspaper. The words in the headline, 'strangled at The Cove with a tie' caught my attention. The Cove is one of my favorite places, but now it won't be anymore."

Scharfkopf, who listened in, was amused. He had told Gigi to improvise if unforeseen questions would come up, and improvise she now did.

Gigi continued, "When driving away from the reunion and Dean told me all that stuff, I didn't take him seriously. But the tie thing did it! When I sat in the dentist's chair, I forgot all about the drilling and concentrated on what I had learned in the waiting room. Later, I googled you and got your address."

She looked the person in the eye and stated, "I figured out what Dean demanded from you for keeping his mouth shut. It wasn't money. Well, *I* definitely want money."

"We can talk about that."

"There is nothing to talk about. I demand $50,000," she prompted. "Meet me here tomorrow with the money."

The person glared at her and stated, "I cannot liquidate that amount on such short notice. You'll have to accept a down payment of $20,000. The rest will have to wait until I move around some assets."

"How long will that take?" asked Gigi.

"A few days."

"Okay. Meet me here again tomorrow at the same time with $20,000 in cash."

"No. It won't be cash. The bank would be on alert if I'd take out that amount in cash. I'll write you a cashier's check."

Gigi said, "There better not be any trouble with cashing it," and getting to her feet, she declared, "See you tomorrow."

CHAPTER 39

Late afternoon on Sunday, Gigi arrived at the San Diego County Sheriff's Department to get unwired. Then she joined Detective Scharfkopf in his office for more briefing.

With a grin on his face he started with, "I'm pleased with your performance today. Well done! You are a natural."

Then he became serious and said, "At the end of your meeting at the mall, one of my 'invisible' team members tailed the perpetrator - - who was in the process of following you - - to the parking garage. The culprit watched from a distance as you pushed the elevator button, then took the stairs. My man was ready to jump into action if you had been threatened, but our criminal observed you getting into your car and then turned around and walked away. I suspect that the perpetrator's objective was to see where your car was parked. People tend to park in approximately the same general areas in malls. So the individual wanted to check out the territory, so to speak, for the next day."

"I never thought about it, but you're right. I usually park on the same level and around the same area at the Mission Valley Mall."

Scharfkopf cleared his throat and continued, "Now let's get to what lies ahead. The reason our suspect checked out your car's location was to form a plan for tomorrow."

"You think the person will place a bomb by my car?" Gigi asked, her eyes as wide as saucers.

"Probably not. It takes time to create an explosive device. One does not purchase the ingredients in a convenience store. You only made your blackmail approach yesterday. No, the plan could include many things. The most likely would be planting a tracking device on your vehicle."

"Then I'd be followed and eliminated when convenient, with no witnesses."

Scharfkopf smiled and said, "A melodramatic way of putting it, but accurate. Remember, we have your back and will not let it come to that. Part of my team will be in the parking garage with unmarked cars and civilian clothing, the rest will be in the vicinity of the theater. I'll be close by too."

He pinned her with an intense stare and stated, "Now is the time to bail out if you're having second thoughts. I won't hold it against you. We do have your conversation with the perpetrator on audio, which can be looked at as admitting guilt, but there is no direct evidence of the crime, and I doubt that what we have would hold up in court. We need to get that $20,000 cashier's check as evidence. Also --"

Gigi interrupted, "You don't have to go on. I'll go ahead and see it through."

"Excellent!"

The phone rang, but he ignored it, letting voicemail kick in, and continued, "I'm sure you realize that the cashier's check for $20,000 is it. Period. There won't be another meeting with the rest of the money."

"I'm aware of that. I may not have a college education, but I have what you call 'street smarts,'" she said.

Scharfkopf grinned. The more he got to know this woman, the more he liked her.

He said, "So tomorrow is D-Day. Come to my office in the late morning and one of my team members will wire you once more. Make sure you wear appropriate clothing again. There may be some last-minute briefing too."

As she got to her feet, he asked, "Your son is staying with your mother. Correct?"

"Yes, and I miss him already," she replied.

CHAPTER 40

The guilty person got to the parking garage ahead of time. Only a few cars were parked in the general area where Gigi would most likely leave her vehicle, since Mondays were the least busy days at the mall. The culprit parked, crouched way down in the driver's seat, and waited.

As expected, when Gigi arrived, she parked her car a few spots away, near the elevator. As soon as she was out of sight, the person made sure that the coast was clear and no other cars were being parked or driven by, then came out of hiding. They carried a can of gasoline with gloved hands over to Gigi's car and poured the liquid out onto the floor beneath her vehicle. Tossing the empty can and the latex gloves into the nearest trash bin, the individual then took the elevator up to the mall.

All seats were empty at the sitting area near the theater, so Gigi had her pick. When she checked her watch and saw that it was five past the hour, she noticed the antagonist approaching.

She said, "I was getting worried that you'd be a no-show."

"Skip the chitchat and let's get this over with," the person hissed, and handed her an envelope with a cashier's check of $20,000.

Gigi looked at it and asked, "I can take this to any bank?"

"Yes."

"I'm going to cash it today and if it doesn't clear, I'm driving straight to the police."

"It will clear."

"When do I get the remaining $30,000?"

"In a few days. Give me your phone number and I'll text you when the assets are available."

Gigi said, "No way am I giving you my number. Remember, I'm the one calling the shots. I'll allow for one week. Meet me here with the rest of the money next Monday at the same time."

That stated, she got up and headed to the elevator.

Seconds later, the culprit used the stairs to the parking garage. Once there, he watched as she stepped inside her car. Then he rushed to it from behind and was about to light an entire matchbook and toss it beneath her vehicle into what logically should have been a puddle of gasoline, when all hell broke loose.

Several law enforcers appeared from behind parked cars, guns drawn, and Detective Scharfkopf's commanding voice droned, "No you don't, Mr. Winter!"

While the matchbook was taken from the perpetrator and dropped into an evidence bag and he was being handcuffed, the detective added, "You thought you were being so clever, killing two birds with one stone. You planned to have the person you thought was your blackmailer and the cashier's check go up in flames. The cashier's check is a nice little piece of evidence and Gigi will be our star witness in court."

Ray Winter was then placed under arrest while the Miranda Rights were being read to him.

CHAPTER 41

Detective Scharfkopf was in no big hurry to interrogate Ray Winter. Let the man stew for a while in his cell, the detective thought. While Ray was being driven to the Sheriff's station by members of his team, he decided that both Gigi and he himself could use some downtime.

He said, "Let me buy you a cup of coffee," and the two took the elevator back up and walked over to the Starbucks situated in the mall.

Once settled with their beverages, she with a cappuccino and he with an espresso, Gigi said, "I don't understand what was happening in the parking garage. I saw Ray approach in the rearview mirror as soon as I sat in my car, but I have no idea what he was up to. Everything happened so fast with your men appearing and the arrest and all. What exactly was he trying to do?"

Scharfkopf stated, "He was planning to blow up your car with you and the cashier's check in it."

"So it was a bomb after all?"

"No. Let me explain. My team got to the parking garage before Winter and watched as he parked his car and then stayed in it, waiting for you to arrive. As soon as you vanished into the elevator, Winter got busy. He emptied an entire can of gasoline under your vehicle. Needless to say that my officers knew that he planned to take a match to it later, before you'd drive away."

Gigi said, "So if you wouldn't have been there to stop him, he'd have succeeded in blowing me up."

"Not exactly. We couldn't take that chance. While you and Winter had your rendezvous upstairs, my team got busy mopping up the gasoline. Even if we hadn't been able to stop him from lighting the matchbox, nothing would have happened to you."

She grinned and stated, "Like you told me, you and your team had my back."

He continued, "The beauty of it is that we have it all on camera. There is a video of him dousing the floor under and around your car with gasoline, as well as at the end, when he pulled that matchbook out of his pocket. In addition we have your testimony and the evidence of his signed cashier's check. All that makes up for a good case and conviction against him. I doubt that even the best of defense lawyers will be able to convince a jury otherwise. If he is smart, he'll confess and that may lessen his prison time."

Gigi took a sip from her cappuccino and then said, "That explains what happened today, but I have other questions. Why did you coach me to tell Ray that Dean didn't blackmail him for money?"

Scharfkopf replied, "That was a shot in the dark but it looks as if I was correct. Dean was a programmer, and I had a hunch that he wanted to get hired at Dercan in their IT department, where Winter was the CIO."

"What about the tie business?" Gigi asked.

"I'm still in the dark about that. Nobody wore a tie when I visited Winter's office the other day, so it couldn't have been a request from the CIO for Dean to show up with a tie."

Gigi went on, "I've been curious about something from the beginning when you asked me to do this undercover thing."

"Shoot."

"You told me that you knew who Dean's murderer was but couldn't prove it. How did you know? I mean, it must have been more than a hunch."

"A few little things captured my attention," he said. "They were not much more than a hunch by themselves. But, put together, they made sense, and I was convinced that Ray Winter was the villain."

He absentmindedly swirled the small amount of espresso that was left in his cup around and continued, "In the beginning I thought that Ray Winter was an unlikely suspect. He did not know Justin Picard personally and met Lori the day after the boy fell from the turret. So he had no connection to either the boy or girl at the time of the tragedy. In other words, he had no motive to kill Justin. During my interview with Winter, he made a major blunder, but I missed it at the time. It was only recently that I caught on.

"My wife and I sat in our travel agent's office and the word 'claustrophobic' came up. It triggered something, and I woke up in the middle of the night remembering what it was. Winter claimed never to have climbed up to the turret yet mentioned that the place was claustrophobic."

Gigi exclaimed, "He couldn't have known that if he'd never gone up."

"Exactly. Why lie about something like that if he was innocent?"

Scharfkopf continued, "I lay awake the rest of the night trying to build a case against Winter. In my own mind I succeeded, but I had no evidence that would hold up in a court of law. For instance, I dwelled on the day I had visited Seabreeze High. When I sat in the teacher's lounge, looking out the window and staring down to the base of the turret, I clearly remembered thinking, from here a person could spot who comes and goes to and from the turret. And the next idea popped into my head: Winter could have sat in the teacher's lounge after teaching the computer class, which was held after school hours.

"Early on in my investigation Sister Margaret remarked that Justin resented her friendship with Lori. In her words, 'He didn't want to share Lori with anyone. He wanted to keep her all to himself.' And while I was awake that night, I recalled a similar comment Winter had made during our interview. He said that now that their twins were in college, he had Lori all to himself again. That statement in itself was harmless, but when it popped into my mind during my sleeplessness, it got me thinking about Ray and Lori's relationship. During my questioning of Lori, I was under the impression that her husband does not want her to go back to work."

People came and went around them and someone accidentally bumped into Gigi's chair, but she hardly noticed, focusing on what the detective was revealing.

He went on, "They met for the first time the day after Justin died, and Ray became her mentor while teaching the class at Seabreeze High. They did not date until Lori was in her second year at UC San Diego. Those are the facts. Winter's protest was genuine when I suggested that he was romantically involved with his future wife during his time at Seabreeze. But what if he had admired her from afar, without her or anyone else noticing? I asked myself. Talking with all suspects, I learned that most boys had had a crush on Lori. There was something special about her, and I think there still is. Her attraction is ageless."

He cleared his throat and said, "I'm getting off the subject here. To make a long story short, during my sleepless night I reconstructed what could have happened the day Justin was killed. And I think I came close to the truth.

"Here goes: Assuming that Ray Winter had been watching Lori from a distance for some time and was obsessed with her, he sat in the teacher's lounge on that fateful early evening and, looking out the window, noticed that Lori and her boyfriend were heading up to the turret. I happen to know that for a fact, since Lori herself told me she broke up with him and left him at the turret the very day he was killed.

"I pictured that a short time later, Ray saw Lori running out of the entrance to the turret alone and clearly upset. I presume that Ray had an idea of what might have happened up there. I deduced that by the time he left the lounge and descended the stairs leading to the lounge, Lori was no longer anywhere near the turret entrance, and he climbed up to it to confront Justin.

"What exactly happened once he came eye to eye with him was guesswork, like everything else I just told you, but it made sense that the two must have engaged in a fistfight. Whether the boy was accidentally thrown over the balustrade of the balcony or whether he was pushed on purpose is so far unclear."

He scratched his head and stated, "I went up to that turret. The railing around the balcony is only about three feet high. It is possible that the boy was flipped over the railing by accident during a physical fight."

Gigi commented, "But in that case, why didn't Ray Winter come forward and say it was an accident?"

"Why indeed? It would have been considered manslaughter, nothing more, and you and I would have never met."

She giggled and added, "Nor sit here having coffee."

Before they each went their separate ways, he thanked her again for a job well done.

CHAPTER 42

On Friday, September 27, Detective Scharfkopf drove to the convent of the Sisters of Temperance, where he faced Sister Margaret in Mother Superior's parlor once more.

He said, "I wanted to see you before you're off to your foreign mission."

"You're in time, I leave early Monday morning."

The detective said, "I want you to know that the case of Dean's murder is solved. Without your help in providing me with a list of suspects, it would have been a lot harder and more time consuming for me to investigate it. So thanks are in order."

He continued, "We arrested Ray Winter, and he confessed to the manslaughter of Justin Picard, the murder of Dean Rickey, and the attempted murder of Gigi. The trial is set for April of next year."

Sister Margaret took a deep breath in and then said, "I will pray for him."

Scharfkopf asked, "You suspected a different person?"

"I did not speculate and refrained from guessing who it could be."

After a pause she asked, "Why did he try to harm Gigi? I mean, she was an outsider and didn't know my classmates; not 30 years ago, nor now."

Without going into details, Scharfkopf explained that he had used Gigi as a mole to lure Winter into action.

"I see."

He chuckled and remarked, "I first thought of you as a plant, but I doubt your Mother Superior would have approved."

A rare smile hushed over Sister Margaret as she said, "She would have forbidden it." She immediately got serious again and declared, "As for me, it would not have offset my guilt."

"What guilt?"

"I blame myself for Dean's death. If I wouldn't have been so self-indulging in getting everyone together for the reunion, Dean would still be alive."

"That's a wrong way of looking at it. You are not to blame for the action of a murderer," he protested.

"Don't you see? Yes, Ray did a horrible thing back at Seabreeze High, but then he lived 30 years as a law-abiding citizen and would have never killed again if it wasn't for the reunion, which I'm responsible for having arranged."

Scharfkopf stated, "All I can say is, you are wrong. Every person is responsible for his own wrongdoing, and any circumstance in regards to someone else is irrelevant."

"My confessor said the same thing," Sister Margaret remarked.

"So believe it and stop feeling guilty."

Then he scratched his head and said, "I know you and Lori are best friends. How did you get along with her husband?" And he quickly added, "I hope this is not too personal a question."

"It is personal, but I'll answer it. On the surface we got along fine, but I've always had the feeling that he resented me. He wanted Lori all to himself."

"On our first interview you told me that Justin had also wanted her to himself."

"Yes," she replied. "There is a pattern."

"You mean possessive boys or men were or are attracted to her?"

"No, that's not what I mean. Most of the opposite sex are attracted to her. It's hard to explain, but I think that whoever Lori was dating or is married to does not want her to share affection with others."

"I'm beginning to understand," he said. "What about Lori herself, is she playing on that?"

"Not at all. She is unaware of it."

After a long pause he said, "Learning that her husband is a murderer must have hit her hard."

Sister Margaret said with conviction, "Yes, that's true, but she's a free spirit and will get over it."

As Scharfkopf got to his feet, he said, "I wish you a safe trip and success with your mission."

"And I wish you happiness in your retirement," said Sister Margaret.

EPILOGUE

One day in the month of July of the following year, Ray Winter sat in his prison cell and wrote a letter. It read:

Dear Lori,

I'm glad you were absent at my trial and have not come to visit me here. I don't think that I'd have the courage to face you. There is no excuse for what I did, but I do think that I owe you an explanation.

Remember when I told you that I wanted you from the first time I saw you? You assumed that was by the bleachers, where I found you crying. True, that had been the first time we spoke, but I admired you from a distance, ever since I'd noticed you cheering for your boyfriend at a football game. Coming across you that day at the bleachers, hurting and vulnerable, you turned to me like you would to an older brother, and I became your mentor. I knew that I had to tread carefully and not reveal my true feelings for you, but as you know, I have a lot of patience.

Here is my confession: On the day that Justin Picard fell from the turret, I sat at the teacher's lounge after teaching the computer class. Looking out the window, I saw you and your boyfriend disappearing into the turret entrance. A short time later, you came running out of there by yourself. Your blouse was torn and you looked clearly distressed. I hurried out of the lounge and ran down the stairs, looking for you, but you were no longer around. Without thinking it through, I headed up to the turret to question Justin. I swear that's all I had in mind, to talk to him.

He was standing at the opening to the balcony when I got there, masturbating. I was full of rage and yelled, "You jerk! I know what you've been up to. Stay away from her." He closed his fly and said, "Mind your own business." That's when I threw my first punch, which started a proper fistfight. He was only a kid of 17 but strong. We were well matched. There was little room on the balcony and the fight took us close to the railing.

Justin ended up being spun over the railing. I honestly don't know whether by accident or if I tossed him over on purpose. Regardless, it would have been manslaughter, not murder, had I notified the police. But I panicked and left the school, not saying a word to anyone. I was sure that there had been no witnesses. The campus was practically empty that late in the day.

My next confession to you is this: I did not get a job offer I could not resist from Dercan. It was the other way around. I contacted them, asking for a position in their company. We couldn't get married while I was a teaching professor at UC San Diego with you as a student there. I didn't want to put off tying the knot until after you graduated. At that point, we had waited long enough.

Now to confession number three: After what happened with Justin, I lived a blameless life for three decades. I had even managed to forget the horrible scene up at the turret. Imagine my shock when listening to Dean Rickey's accusation. There was no doubt in my mind that he was out to blackmail me. I followed him outdoors when he took a cigarette break and asked him point blank what he wanted. The bastard was not your regular blackmailer, asking for money. Oh no! He wanted a job at Dercan as Director of Technology, in my department, no less.

There was no way I could allow that to take place. Blackmailers never stop after the first payoff. Dean would have had demand after demand in the future, possibly ending with taking over my own job as CIO. He also seemed the type who tried to make himself important. Why else would he have made his accusation in front of the entire group? What guarantee did I have that he would keep his mouth shut if I gave in to his demand? No. I had to come up with a quick plan to eliminate him.

Looking at the nerd, puffing on his cigarette and wearing the silly bow tie, I thought, if he wore a regular necktie it could be used to strangle him. And in a flash, I came up with a plan. I pretended to go along with his demand and told him not to worry about coming to the office for a job interview but to meet me at The Cove the next morning, where we could iron out the details. He was eager to agree and I said, "A bow tie seems to be your trademark, but if you report to me and are responsible for various information technology teams, I insist that you wear a regular tie. Bring one with you tomorrow, so that I can see for myself that you're capable of tying a proper knot."

All nonsense, of course. People are no longer required to wear ties in the workplace in California, especially not in the IT department. But Dean didn't know that and accepted it as the truth. He said that he'd packed one if needed for a job interview.

Before I went back to our table, I made a stop at the men's room. After all, that was supposedly why I left the reunion hall. While washing my hands, I came up with the idea for an alibi for Sunday morning and left my wedding band behind on purpose. I figured that it would be a matter of a minute or so to drive from the hotel to the parking lot near The Cove, and I would make sure to exchange a few words with the hotel concierge when retrieving my ring.

That night, after you had dozed off to sleep, I lay awake a bit longer and fine-tuned my plan. One thing was to make sure to leave my shoes in the car before heading out to the beach. I didn't want to leave footprints in the sand, and it would also be a precaution in case my shoes would later on be examined for sand residue.

Well, you need not have been present at my trial to know what happened at The Cove the following morning. It was on the news and in the local papers. I did have a moment's hesitation before the actual strangulation. Dean told me that he didn't in fact see me throw Justin from the turret but only witnessed me coming from the entry leading up to it at the crucial day and time. He also told me the motive, namely that I wanted you to myself. This sounded far-fetched, since you and I didn't get married until years later. But it was the truth and who knew what a jury would do with it.

In the same breath, he also admitted that blackmailing me hadn't just occurred to him the evening before, but that he had planned it before leaving Arizona. He had googled people who would be at the reunion, especially the ones who had not been to any previous ones, ahead of time. On learning that I was married to you, he realized he had a golden opportunity to get what he was after.

These facts put an end to my hesitation and I executed what I had come to The Cove to do.

To my final confession concerning Gigi: I had underestimated the young woman, having no clue that she'd been planted by Detective Scharfkopf. That man outsmarted me in the end. He somehow had figured me out but had no proof and decided to use a layperson as a pretend second blackmailer to get a reaction out of me. His plan worked. Gigi acted her part to perfection. I looked at her as I had judged her on the night of the reunion, namely a pretty airhead, working for an escort service.

I believed her story that Dean had revealed me to her and took her for a blackmailer. Demanding $50,000 seemed about right for someone in her position. Anyway, I will not bore you with the details, you may know them already. Suffice it to say that I was in the process of blowing up her car with her and my cashier's check in it, when Scharfkopf's people stopped me.

This concludes my confession.

I hope that you were as happy in our marriage as I. Thank you for 27 years of bliss, my dear Lori. The first seven years, before we had the twins, were paradise. Now that the twins are away at college, I was looking forward to only you and me again, but I messed that up big time.

It is a fact that I will never get out of prison alive and I'm trying to come to terms with that reality. I do hope that you and the twins will find it in your hearts to forgive me, which would make it easier to tolerate.

With all my love,

Ray.

He reread the letter, then stared at it for a long time, not sure if he was ever going to mail it. Then he glanced at his prison cell with the bars across the door, the pitiful bunk bed, and the even more pitiful toilet in the corner.

He told himself, *I should have put my foot down and not attended that doomed reunion.*

Stand-Alone Mysteries by Alice Zogg

A Doomed Reunion
A Lethal Joke
A Dark Book Club
A Bad Apple
Exposing the Past
No Curtain Call
The Ill-Fated Scientist
Accidental Eyewitness
A Bet Turned Deadly

R. A. Huber Mysteries by Alice Zogg

Evil at Shore Haven
Guilty or Not
Murder at the Cubbyhole
Revamp Camp
Final Stop Albuquerque
The Fall of Optimum House
The Lonesome Autocrat
Tracking Backward
Turn the Joker Around
Reaching Checkmate

www.ingramcontent.com/pod-product-compliance
Lightning Source LLC
Chambersburg PA
CBHW052136170626
46812CB00004B/1447